BLESSED BETRAYAL

LIVIA GRANT

Blessed Betrayal
©2018 Livia Grant

eBook ISBN: 978-1-947559-00-4
Print ISBN: 978-1-947559-01-1
Cover art by: Laura Hidalgo at Book Fabulous Design
Editor: Sandy Ebel at Personal Touch Editing

This book is a work of fiction. While reference might be made to actual historical events or existing locations, the names, characters, places, and incidents are either the product of the author's imagination or are used fictitiously, and any resemblance to actual persons, living or dead, business establishments, events, or locales is entirely coincidental.

Published in the United States of America

Livia Grant

http://www.liviagrant.com/

Blurb:

> She wanted happily ever after.
> He thought he had it.

Underneath the perfect exterior of Calista Bennett's marriage lay an ugly truth that threatens to drown her when she is betrayed.

Across town, Nickolas Mikos isn't doing much better after his life is plunged into his new reality by his wife's lies.

Life can change in the blink of an eye. Can Cali and Nick comfort each other's raw pain enough to allow for a second chance at happiness, or will their fears and anger prevent them from uncovering the blessing in the betrayal?

I'm sorry, Cali. I know it isn't what you wanted to hear, but the test was negative."

Her hopeful apprehension morphed to dread. "Are you sure? Should we do another?"

Dr. Galloway smiled indulgently. "That won't be necessary. The tests are very reliable. I'm sure you took one at home as well, didn't you?"

"Yes." Her dejected reply was barely a whisper.

"Then you already know taking it again would just be a waste." The OBGYN doctor wheeled his rolling stool closer to the exam table to pat Cali's knee in a fatherly way. "I know you and your husband are anxious to get your family started, but you're only twenty-four. You have plenty of time. We have a lot of options we haven't tried yet."

Cali struggled to hold back her tears. How could she tell her kind doctor how important it was for her to get pregnant?

"I think it's time for us to do testing on your husband. Since we haven't found any smoking gun on your side of the equation, it's time to take a look at Mr. Bennett's sperm count and mobility. That will help me decide our next steps."

"I don't know about that, Dr. Galloway. Kevin is so busy with his job. He joined his father's law firm last year and is working crazy hours. I doubt he can come in for an appointment." Cali didn't know how to tell the good doctor her husband had made it very clear giving him an heir was her responsibility, and the only help he planned contributing to the process was a *'daily hard fuck.'* The array of bruises scattered across her body were proof he was living up to his *hard* promise.

Calista trembled as she realized her temporary veil of protection had fallen with the negative test result. Kevin was gentler with her during the weeks of the month she might be in the process of forming a fragile new life. For the last year, each month the results were negative, he not only deemed it his responsibility to punish her for failing him yet again, but he then proceeded to make up for lost time. The next two weeks of her life were going to be hell.

No. She couldn't tell the kind doctor that.

"What would he have to do?"

"Us men have it pretty easy, to be honest," the doctor grinned wolfishly. "You poor women get poked and prodded with all kinds of needles and drugs. Your husband just needs to come in and give us a deposit of his sperm. He'll have a private room and will be able to bring along reading or viewing material he might need to help. All in all, the men have it pretty good in this deal."

How right he was. "Okay, I'll talk to him about it."

"Sounds good. Keep your chin up. We've done a lot of tests, and I see no reason why you can't get pregnant. It's gonna happen when the time is right and not a minute before."

"Thanks again, doctor." She forced a smile to hide her growing sense of dread. "I'll see you next time."

As Calista redressed, she said a small prayer that Kevin would be in a good mood when he got home today. He'd been out of town on business the last two days. Since passing the bar exam, he'd been working eighty hours a week or more, and in truth, he was gone so much, it made her life less stressful most of the time. Unfortunately, he still checked in at home often enough to dump his dirty laundry and contribute his duty to operation 'give me an heir.'

Sitting at a stop light on the drive home, Cali once again questioned why she stayed with her husband. He'd changed so much since they got married almost two years before. He had always been dominant... demanding. The problem was he'd begun to take the definition of dominant to a whole new level. Cali used to think of herself as a submissive. Lately, she felt more like a well-worn doormat.

Cali was just doing a final check of her makeup in the large vanity mirror when she heard the garage door opening one floor below. She had taken extra care in her preparations for tonight's Bennett, Bennett, and Moore post-holiday party. She knew how important it was to her husband.

She may not have understood why Kevin had singled her out when they'd met during her senior year at the University of Virginia, but she certainly knew now. Cali had been flattered when the president of the university's most prominent law organization had set his sights on her. As a final year law student, he'd been charming, sweeping her off her feet with gifts, assurances of love, and romantic gestures.

Now, a few years later, she knew what a mistake she had made believing a single word he'd said. He had made it abundantly clear after she had said her 'I dos,' she was his showpiece. His grandfather and father were managing partners in one of Washington D.C.'s most prestigious law firms, specializing in international tax law. The fact Kevin had the last name Bennett had assured her husband a top spot at the large firm straight out of law school. It also meant she was married to a man who had unlimited resources to make her life a living hell should she try to leave him. She ought to know. She had tried. Just once, a year ago. She'd learned first-hand as ugly as it was being married to him, trying to leave him was worse.

Cali had been lost in thought, missing his arrival in their master suite. She caught his reflection in the mirror as he stood in the doorway. Her stomach churned at the sight of his predatory glare that reminded her of a hunter, about to pounce on his prey.

"You're as gorgeous as ever, my dear. I see you took my advice and wore red." His words may have been complimentary, but they didn't distract Cali from the danger just under the surface of his handsome exterior. He had proven his mood could change on a dime.

"Of course, I wore red. I didn't think it was a suggestion, rather an order."

"Of course, it was an order." He took deliberate steps closer, never taking his eyes from her reflection. "But an obedient wife wouldn't be so crass as to point out that distinction. I keep warning you, Calista. You're being groomed. You're not going to hear other partner's wives talking in that tone tonight. You'd do well to watch and learn, my dear."

He had stepped up behind her as she sat at the make-up mirror, resting his manicured hands on her bare shoulders. His touch was deceptively gentle. She never forgot how hard those hands could turn when he was angered which was why she had made it her new life's mission to keep him as happy as possible. Just like a good little wife.

"Yes, sir. I'll remember that."

"You do that. What a shame. It looks like you're almost ready. I had hoped to fit in a little *exercise* before we left for the party."

She hated to *exercise* with her husband. It was his code word for delivering her *'daily hard fuck.'* She had hoped he would delay at least until after the party if she was already dressed.

"I wanted to be ready when you got home. I know how much you hate to be late."

"How thoughtful of you." His steely blue eyes were cooling. "And here I was thinking it was because you didn't want to tell me the results of your appointment this afternoon."

Cali's heart was thundering so hard, she felt the pounding in her ears. She froze with panic, made worse as Kevin's hands slid from her shoulders to circle her throat, slowly constricting until she had to fight for her next breath. She pushed against the marble countertop in a feeble attempt to free herself from his grip, but he pressed her forward, making her thrashing futile. Her husband cut off her airflow until she began to see stars, finally releasing her while leaning down to whisper menacingly into her ear.

"You're such a disappointment to me, Calista."

Cali gasped, filling her lungs with precious air, hating the tears streaming down her cheeks from the exertion. Trails of dark mascara marred the reflection of the beautiful woman with long black hair staring back at her from the mirror.

"I only ask one thing of you." His quiet rage was simmering hotter. "I plucked you out of poverty and gave you the life of a princess. Yet you insist on keeping that ridiculous job teaching other people's children when what

5

you should be focused on is providing me with the child I need to fulfill the requirements in my grandfather's will. He hasn't been well, and I'm going to hold you responsible if the old man kicks it before I have time to claim my share of the pie with an heir."

Fear helped her fight down the urge to remind him she was trying to create a baby, not an heir. "I was disappointed too, Kevin. I was late this month, and I really did think we had a chance." Cali should have stopped there. "Dr. Galloway wants you to make an appointment to come in to be tested as well. He needs your test results to decide what the next course of action should be."

Cali knew immediately she had made a grave error. Kevin's blue eyes had turned to ice, venom flowing from them.

"How dare you blame me for this, you bitch? You have one fucking job in this marriage, and when you can't get it done, you decide to put the blame on me?"

"No... that's not... I mean it's just..." Her voice quavered. "It's a formality, that's all. The doctor does this with all couples who have problems conceiving."

He wasn't placated. "Like I have time to go in to be poked and prodded. I'll be damned if I'm going to turn into a pin cushion because you can't do your job."

She wanted to scream that everyone knew it took two to create a child, but she wisely kept that retort to herself.

"He promised you wouldn't be poked or prodded. It's easy for the men. You'll just need to give a sperm sample."

"Ah, is that all? I just need to go jack off behind some lame curtain like a lab rat? Well, no thanks. I provide sperm samples each and every day I fuck you. In fact, I missed a day yesterday. I think you need a reminder of exactly how frequently I have provided sperm samples in this marriage."

She should have been prepared, but she hadn't expected

things to escalate so quickly. Kevin gripped her biceps in a vice grip and yanked her to her feet just long enough to smash her body forward. She was sprawled across the marble countertop, her forehead smashed against the over-sized mirror. Cali squeezed her eyes closed, trying to shut out the vision of her husband's icy eyes as she felt him flipping the skirt of her dress over her back just before he ripped the lacy underwear from her body. He insisted she wear stockings and garter belts with skirts, so she was now bare.

It only took him a few seconds to fumble with his zipper before she felt his hard erection spring free. It was inside her in one hard thrust. She was grateful she'd been careful to lube both her pussy and ass thoroughly after her shower. She had learned the hard way to make sure her body was prepared at a moment's notice to take Kevin's punishing cock.

She tried so hard to hold back the scream but failed miserably. His responding chuckle reminded her she was married to a sadist.

As he set a fast pace, Cali's fight turned internal. As much as her brain hated what he did to her and how he made her feel, there was no denying her body betrayed her time and again. Kevin liked to use the natural lubrication flowing copiously from her body as proof she actually liked to be treated like his punching bag. Cali may have started to hate her husband, but she hated her own body more.

He fucked her like a machine, pistoning her to her first humiliating climax. She lay limp across the counter, receiving all he gave her, his ridiculing laughter only raising her humiliation. She was too lost in her orgasmic fog to recognize the few second intermission in the action. The piercing pain of his cock shoved balls-deep in her lubed rectum consumed her. She barely made out his grunting words.

"Lucky you lubed yourself. This would have hurt like a bitch if you'd forgotten."

Cali lay boneless, receiving her hard fuck of the day, knowing it was unfortunately early enough there was a good chance he might go for round two when they got home from the party. She had learned the trick to surviving this particular *exercise* was to relax into it. Her husband had grabbed her hips, gripping her hard enough, she was sure he was leaving fresh bruises over the faded ones from past *exercise* sessions.

They were in a race. Her body was beginning to betray her again. She couldn't fight him, but she went to work, waging war against herself, trying desperately to hold back her orgasm, not wanting to give him the satisfaction of dragging it from her.

He didn't play fair. He leaned down and pressed his chest to her back. She wasn't fooled into thinking he wanted the added intimacy of their sweaty skin caressing each other. No. He only did this so he could reach her clit with his left hand. He wasn't trying to bring her satisfaction, rather humiliation as her body exploded into another strong climax. He joined her a minute later, collapsing on her, almost cutting off her breath again. He added salt to her wounds as she lay recovering.

"That's the only good thing about you not being pregnant. We have a few weeks before I need to start making deposits in your pussy again. I do love taking this ass of yours. It's nice and tight, just the way I like it." He pulled out as abruptly as he had inserted, slapping her ass with his open palm while stepping away from her. "I'm gonna take a shower. Put yourself back together. We'll leave in thirty minutes."

He didn't wait for her answer. He didn't need to. He knew she was too afraid to do anything but what he asked.

CHAPTER 2

*N*ick pulled his BMW into the cramped carport of The Jefferson Hotel. Just a few blocks north of the White House, the hotel was one of the most prestigious in the city. The stately doorman opened his door, welcoming them to the historic property. Nick looked over the employee's shoulder to see a homeless man propped up against the building across the street. The man was shivering in the freezing cold January evening. The dichotomy of wealth and poverty were never far from each other in this part of town.

Nick circled the car, stopping to assist his wife from the low riding vehicle. He had offered to drive the family van so she would be more comfortable, but she'd looked at him as if he were from Mars.

We can't show up to a Bennett, Bennett, and Moore event in a van, Nicholas.

He took his wife's elbow as he moved them to the door held wide by yet another employee. Only now did he recognize Veronica was in a fur coat he had never seen before. Between the coat, designer dress, and new shoes, he wondered how much tonight's free dinner was costing him.

They made their way through the elegant lobby and past cozy seating areas where some of the country's numerous back-door business deals had been cut over a cocktail and a cigar.

The overt opulence turned Nick's stomach. It was an in-his-face reminder of the cultural philosophy of the law firm where he had been employed for the eight years he had been a lawyer. Now was not the time to reflect on how he had ended up at this point in his career, questioning everything he'd been fighting for. He had mistakenly thought working for the largest international law firm in the nation's capital might afford him the chance to help those less fortunate around the globe. Instead, he more often found himself representing those who would exploit the most helpless of the world.

If it weren't for his wife, he would have left years before. Appearances and status symbols ruled Veronica's life, and he was under no disillusion. If he left BB&M to work at one of the many non-profit global organizations he longed to represent, he was certain his marriage would be over. If he only had himself to worry about, he might take the chance of going it alone, but he didn't want to put his baby girl through an ugly divorce. Although if things kept on the declining trajectory at the firm, he might not have a choice soon.

"Oh my God, look at the chandeliers!" Veronica managed to keep her profile regal while whispering excitedly under her breath so only he could hear her. "They are amazing. I think one of them would look good above our dining room table."

"You would like them. I'm sure just one would cost a fortune."

She didn't let the smile slip from her lips, but he saw the ice in her eyes as she responded. "If you'd press harder for that promotion to partner, Nicholas, we could afford a hell of a lot more than just a chandelier."

"Roni, this is not the time or the place for this discussion. I told you there are extenuating circumstances. There is no chance I'll be offered an associate partnership, and honestly, even if they offered, I'd turn it down, and you know it."

Her polished exterior was cracking as she spat her reply, "For the thousandth time, stop calling me Roni in public. I hate it, and you know it."

Nick sighed. Not this ridiculous argument again. They approached the entrance to the prestigious dining room where the sixty employees of the firm and their significant others were about to have their annual holiday party. The room was barely large enough to seat the group, round-tops arranged in a too-close pattern. They stopped at a table with tented seating assignment cards arranged in alphabetical order. He moved to the M's for Mikos, expecting to find a high number. After the argument they'd had just yesterday, he was sure George Bennett would want him seated as far away from the head partner's table as possible.

Veronica found the card first. "Oh, how exciting! They have us seated at table two. We're almost seated at the head table!"

She was practically dragging him behind her as she weaved them through the packed tables toward the front of the room. They were almost there when Nick recognized who else would be seated at their table. He pulled his wife to a stop.

"Hold on, Veronica. There has to be a mistake. That can't be our table. Let's go back to the door and see if there's another table we can take."

"Are you kidding me?" She trained her angry eyes on him. "You're finally moving up the ladder, and you're gonna screw it up. We always get stuck in the back. It's our turn to sit at the front of the room, Nicholas."

Unwilling to make a scene, he allowed his wife to pull him along behind her. There were two couples already seated at table two. He recognized one as George Bennett's attractive personal assistant, Tamara and her husband. It was the other couple who had Nick wishing he could sit at the back of the room. The farther he could sit away from George Bennett's blow-hard son, Kevin, the better.

From the minute they'd met, there had been no love lost between the men. The youngest Bennett to join the firm was the worst of them all. At least his two older brothers attempted to earn their seat at the family table. Kevin had only been out of law school a year and already treated every person he met at the firm like gum stuck to the bottom of his shoe.

"Mikos. How'd you end up sitting way up here? I'd have thought you'd be more comfortable sitting with the wait staff in the employee cafeteria. Maybe you could help them negotiate for a dime an hour raise."

"Sounds like more fun than spending the next few hours with you, Bennett. Looks like your father has a sense of humor, putting us together."

Tamara started to speak, "But Mr. Bennett, I thought..."

She didn't get to finish her sentence. Her words froze under the icy stare sent her way by the youngest Bennett. She actually shuddered under his glare. Tamara's husband hugged her to silently comfort her.

Veronica moved in to take the open seat next to Kevin before Nick could move them to the back of the room. She acted as if she was oblivious to the chill in the air between the men. Nick weighed his options. Deciding not to make a scene, he took the last seat at the table.

Once seated, he couldn't help but notice the beautiful

woman sitting directly across the small table. By process of elimination, she had to be with Kevin, yet he hadn't bothered to introduce her. Typical.

Turning first to Tamara, he reached out to shake hands with her husband. "Nicholas Mikos. This is my wife, Veronica."

"Nice to meet you, Nicholas. James, Tamara's husband."

"You as well." Nick moved his gaze around the table until he was looking into the most exquisite amber-brown eyes he had ever seen. He momentarily lost the ability to speak as he took in the natural beauty of the olive-skinned woman who looked so uncomfortable. It seemed she would like to be seated at the back of the room as well.

"It would appear Kevin has forgotten his manners. I'm going to assume you are his wife. As you heard, I'm Nicholas Mikos, and this is my wife, Veronica. I work with your husband."

"For."

It was the only word Kevin had injected into the introduction process. Nick turned to question him when he got his answer.

"You work *for* me, not *with* me."

What a pretentious prick. Nick did the only thing he could do under the circumstances—laughed his ass off. By the time he got his laughter under control, he could feel the grip of Veronica's hand squeezing his thigh under the table and could see the steam rolling out of the ears of the young blow-hard to their left.

"Thanks for the laugh, Bennett. You're so green, you don't even know how ridiculous you sound going around making stupid statements like that."

"Green? We'll see how green I am when I get your ass fired. You're already on thin ice with my father."

"You're digging yourself deeper every time you open your

mouth. Let me help you out. You're right, your father and I often bump heads on the right course of action for our clients, but I know for a fact, your father respects me for my conviction. Even if he didn't, the fact I've billed high six-figures for the last three years in a row is making him... and unfortunately you... a very rich man."

"I think we should change the subject. It's nice to meet you, Nicholas and Veronica. I'm Kevin's wife, Calista, but you can call me Cali."

Nick had almost forgotten the woman he had been addressing until she quietly tried to interject. No doubt, she was trying to save her husband from looking like more of an asshole than he already had.

It didn't work.

"How many times have I told you I hate when you shorten your name? You're Calista. Period. Cali sounds like a name for someone's cat."

"Oh thank goodness, someone else who has some sense," Veronica globbed on. "Nicholas insists on calling me Roni, and I hate it."

Anger he hadn't felt in a long time flared up in Nick. It was bad enough he had to put up with shit from the prick at the table, but not his wife, too.

"Well, it's nice to meet you, Cali. I'd love it if you'd call me Nick." She managed to squelch the smile playing at her lips, but she couldn't hide the humor in her eyes at his barb at their spouses.

The next hour was painful. Conversation at the table was often strained with Kevin and Veronica doing most of the talking. He knew the young Bennett was purposefully flirting with his wife who was status hungry enough to lap up his attention. He should have been angry, but the most prevalent emotion he felt was relief at not having to carry a conversation with the asshole. Instead, he chatted with

Tamara's husband about golf and local sports teams. He tried several times to include Cali in the conversation, but she spent most of the time sitting quietly, looking down at her hands clasped in her lap. Nick couldn't shake the feeling something wasn't quite right in the young woman's marriage. Knowing whom she was married to, it made sense.

Tamara tried to keep the table talk on safe ground. "Who is watching your daughter tonight, Mr. Mikos?"

Nick's mood improved at the mention of the daughter he loved more than anything else in the world. "She's staying overnight at her best friend's house. She's always happy to have an excuse for a sleepover."

He didn't miss his wife's quiet dig under her breath. "She's not the only one."

His anger flared. Nick reached and squeezed her thigh as a warning. These anti-motherhood comments of hers were getting tiresome. He had always known Roni wasn't interested in competing for the mother-of-the-year award, but recently, she'd been downright ambivalent about any activity that included their adorable seven-year-old daughter, Andrea. He used to think Veronica's indifference to Andi was because she was jealous of how close he was with his only child, but it felt deeper these last few months. He'd tried to talk to her about it, of course, and things would improve for a day or two, but just long enough for Nick to know it was an act.

Kevin berating Cali brought Nick's attention back to the table. He picked up on the prick's slurred words, proving he'd already overindulged in the freely flowing champagne.

"Wouldn't it be great if we had a little one to be going to sleepovers, Calista? Oh, that's right, we won't get to enjoy that, will we, since you can't seem to perform your wifely duty."

Nick saw a shiver pass through Cali before she quietly answered her husband. "Please, Kevin. Not here. Not now."

He backed down. "You're absolutely right. We'll have a nice long *talk* about it when we get home, won't we?" Those words brought a full tremble to Kevin's wife.

The table fell quiet again. Nick wanted to deck the jerk but settled for sending Kevin a threatening stare until the ass seemed to realize he'd gone too far.

After the dinner plates had been cleared, Veronica rose to excuse herself. "I'll be back in a few minutes. Be a dear, Nicholas, and order me a coffee."

Looking relieved that dinner was over, Tamara and James took the opportunity to get up and mingle, leaving Nick with the unhappy couple. He was about to rise to follow his wife to the restrooms when Kevin stood, abruptly leaving the table without even a word to his wife.

Nick was reluctant to leave Cali alone at the table even if her own husband didn't seem to care. They sat alone in silence for several uncomfortable minutes before Cali broke the silence.

"You're different from most of the other men who work at Bennett, Bennett, and Moore," she said quietly as if she didn't want her father-in-law at the next table to hear her.

Nick wished she would look up so he could see those golden eyes again. "I'll take that as a compliment, Mrs. Bennett."

"Cali." She finally gazed up into his eyes, speaking with sincerity. "And that's good because I meant it as a compliment."

There was a sadness about her that wouldn't go away even when she smiled.

"I have a question for you, Cali, but I'm afraid it's impolite and inappropriate under the circumstances. Still, I'd like to ask."

She hesitated, her beautiful eyes widening at his request. Her answer was quiet. "You can ask, I don't know if I'll answer."

Nick smiled kindly. "You're a beautiful woman, Cali, and you seem like a very nice person. How the hell did you end up married to a prick like Kevin Bennett?"

He regretted asking immediately. Cali's quiet sadness turned to panic. She looked around to see if anyone at the nearby tables was listening to their conversation. Her shoulders slumped only slightly when it appeared as if they weren't being spied on. Still, she didn't answer the question. It hung in the air long enough, he wondered if she'd ever talk to him again.

When her eyes met his again, the sadness was back. "Funny, I've wanted to ask you the same thing, Nick."

Nick sighed, understanding that everyone had to walk their own path. There were times he wished things had turned out differently too, but then he thought of Andi, and his doubts vanished.

It was late by the time the party wrapped up. Nick steered Veronica to mingle with other partygoers when she returned from the restroom, salvaging the rest of the night. When they returned to their table to pick up Roni's clutch purse, Cali was gone. Nick saw her at the head table, listening to her mother-in-law babble non-stop. Sensing his eyes on her, she looked up, a sad smile on her lips. Nick wished he could ease her sadness, but there was nothing he could do. He nodded in her direction before turning to follow Roni to the exit.

CHAPTER 3

*C*ali lowered herself slowly into the driver's seat of her sedan. The over-the-counter pain medication she had taken that morning had long since worn off, leaving her body aching. As much as she hurt today, she was still better than yesterday. She had called in sick the day before, for the first time in her two years of teaching third grade at Franklin Elementary school, electing to stay home to give her strained muscles time to recover. She'd been achy all day, but her co-workers just thought she was still recovering from the aftermath of the flu. They never needed to know it was the aftermath of an especially long and strenuous Kevin Bennett *exercise* session that had her in pain.

The drive from the school to their upscale suburban home was gratefully short. In fact, in better weather, Cali liked to walk to and from work.

The house was quiet when she entered the kitchen through the garage. She didn't expect her husband home until much later that night. Luckily, he'd been out of town on business the night before, allowing her body a night off to recover. She knew better than to hope he would be detained another night.

Life had been particularly hellish in the two weeks since her last visit to the doctor. She prayed this was the month she would get pregnant. Things would be so much better once they had a baby on the way.

At first, Cali hadn't understood Kevin's big rush to have kids, but she had since found out the details of her grandfather-in-law's will. The man was as egocentric as they came, wanting to leave behind a legacy of decedents. It was so important to him his grandchildren would inherit shares of the sizable estate based on the size of their families. Considering they already lived in a house much too big and owned three vehicles for two people, Cali didn't understand her husband's urgency to get a bigger piece of the family pie.

Once upstairs, she swallowed another dose of Tylenol before slipping into a steaming hot bath until the ache of her muscles had eased.

After her bath, Cali fixed a simple grilled cheese sandwich, settling into grade papers and read a book. The sound of her cell phone startled her. It was his ring.

"Hello, Kevin."

"Hey. I'm gonna be stuck here another night. I won't be home until tomorrow night now."

Conflicting emotions invaded. Relief won. "That's too bad. I haven't taken my ovulation test yet, but it's gonna be any day. Do you think you'll be home tomorrow night?"

"Yes, Calista. I'll be home tomorrow night in time to service you properly. I haven't forgotten my duty as sperm donor."

His words sparked her anger. She was always so much braver over the phone than when he was there in person.

"Do you even hear yourself? We're married, Kevin. I'm

your wife. I think you're supposed to be a little more than just a damn sperm donor in my life."

"Dammit, Calista, I'm not going to have this discussion over the phone."

"If not over the phone, then when?"

She heard a shuffle at his end. "Listen Calista, I know things have been kind of rough for us these last few months. I have my reasons for being so stressed. You're right. We should talk when I get home tomorrow." He spoke in the gentlest voice she had heard in months. It reminded her of the Kevin she had been in love with once.

Hot tears prickled. She was tired of being afraid. She wanted to trust her husband. "I'd like that Kevin. We can't go on like this anymore. Things have to change."

He was quiet long enough, she'd begun to think they'd been disconnected.

"I can't do this right now, Cali. I should be home early tomorrow. Why don't we go out to Rivers for dinner?"

Damn him. Just when she had her protective walls built around her heart, he would show her a glimpse of the Kevin she had thought she was marrying. His split personality seemed to be on the same biological clock as her menstrual cycle. Two weeks of hellish rutting followed by two weeks of making love. Her heart was developing a case of whiplash.

"I'd love that, Kevin."

"Go to bed. I'll see you tomorrow." He didn't wait for her reply, the call dropped.

It took her a few minutes to realize what was so different about their exchange. It was the first time he had called her Cali in months... even in private.

She dozed off thinking of how happy she had been when he had proposed at Rivers over two years ago and how much had changed since that magical night. Could they get back some of that magic tomorrow night?

The sound of a bell ringing, followed by a pounding jarred Cali awake. The dark bedroom was quiet. Her husband's half of the bed was still empty. What had she been dreaming about that had woken her so abruptly?

She looked at the alarm clock on the bed stand. It read 4:04 a.m. She took a few calming breaths to settle her nerves. She was just lying down to try to get back to sleep when the doorbell rang.

Panic invaded. They lived in a safe neighborhood, but did someone know she was home alone tonight? Who could be at the door at this hour?

She knew Kevin had a handgun somewhere in the house, but she'd never learned how to use it. She jumped up and ran to the window facing the front of the house, pulling the gauze drape aside enough to peek out.

Panic turned to dread as she saw a police car in the driveway. Her mind raced to think of possible reasons for a visit by the police at this hour. Each scenario seemed worse than the one before. She rushed to her closet to grab her terrycloth robe before she jogged to the stairs, turning on the lights to the entryway to alert the police she was awake. The in-progress knocking stopped immediately.

Cali looked out the peephole. Standing on her porch were two uniformed police officers. They looked official, but she was still afraid. She wished Kevin were home with her to handle this.

She didn't want to open the door. "Hello, officers. It's late. What's the problem?"

She watched through the viewer as the taller of the two responded to her question. "We're sorry to disturb you at this hour ma'am, but there's been an accident. We'd like to come in to discuss it with you."

An accident. Her first thought went to her father. She hadn't talked to him in months. "An accident? Was it my father?"

"Honestly, ma'am, we're not sure. If you'd open the door, we have a few questions for you. Perhaps you could help us sort things out."

Cali took a deep breath and unlocked the front door. A blanket of dread surrounded her as she let the two officers into the foyer. The shorter, stockier man reached out his hand with a business card.

"I'm Officer Jackson, and this is my partner, Officer Stanton. If you don't mind me asking, who might you be?"

The question was unexpected. They were standing in her foyer. Surely, they knew who she was. "I'm Calista Bennett."

She didn't miss the quick glance between the men before Officer Jackson spoke.

"And who is Kevin Bennett to you, ma'am?"

"Is Kevin in some type of trouble officer?"

"Just answer the question if you would, ma'am."

Cali's voice quavered in her reply. "Kevin's my husband, but he's out of town on business this week. He'll be back tomorrow afternoon if you need to speak with him. What is this about again?"

It was Officer Stanton who spoke, "Perhaps we could sit down before we answer your questions."

Panic had her heart pounding in her ears. "I don't want to sit down. I just want to know why you're here."

Officer Stanton's eyes filled with pity before he spoke.

"I'm sorry to tell you this, Mrs. Bennett, but we believe your husband was in an accident a few hours ago." He stopped long enough to take a small notebook out of the front pocket of his bulletproof vest. Flipping the pages, he finally continued, "Does your husband own a silver 2016 Audi R8?"

Her answer was a whispered, "Yes. It was a graduation gift from his parents when he passed the bar." The truth was sinking in. Kevin had been in an accident. "Let me go change my clothes. What hospital did they take him to?" Only then did Cali realize he hadn't even shared what city he was in. "He's on a business trip. Where do I need to go to see him?"

The officers hesitated. "I'm sorry to inform you that your husband died from his injuries."

Cali would have collapsed to the floor if Officer Stanton hadn't caught her. He let her lean on him heavily as he steered her to the nearby living room. They sat on the closest love seat, and he wrapped his arm around her as unconscious tears overflowed down her cheeks. Her mind reeled. There had to be a mistake.

"Where did this happen?"

"On Interstate 395 headed into the city. Do you know where he might have been heading?"

"No! I told you. He's out of town." Relief invaded. She turned hopeful eyes on the officer. "Someone must have stolen his car! It had to be someone else in the car. Let me phone him."

"I'm sorry, but we're almost certain it was your husband driving." The pity in his eyes had grown stronger. "He had his identification on him, and they were able to identify him at the scene from his driver's license photo. Of course, the coroner will make absolutely certain in the autopsy."

"Autopsy? Wait. I don't believe it. It can't be Kevin! I just talked to him a few hours ago. We're going to Rivers tomorrow night for dinner." Her voice had taken on a manic quality as her tears increased.

"We normally don't recommend family members identify their loved ones when the bodies have been traumatized by high-speed accidents, but we honestly would appreciate it if you could accompany us to the morgue."

He hesitated long enough that Officer Jackson completed the request, "I'm afraid your husband wasn't alone in the car at the time of the accident. His companion didn't have any identification in the vehicle they were able to find on the scene. If you feel up to it, we could sure use your help in identifying the other victim of the accident."

Other victim. Accident. Cali's mind reeled. It was hard for her to focus. Had he been trying to come home tonight after all? If so, why had he been going in the wrong direction? And who was in the car with him? The officers gave her time to mull the devastating news around long enough, she started to formulate her own suspicions.

"It was a woman?" she finally asked although it came out as more of a statement.

"I'm afraid so, ma'am. We came here unsure if anyone would be here. We thought perhaps it had been you in the car with him. Is there anyone else you can think of he might have been with around midnight?"

Cali knew. She just knew. Still, it didn't make it easier to say, "No one he should have been with, no."

"I know it will be difficult, but could you please help us identify the other victim? We'd like to notify her next of kin."

Cali wanted to tell them she didn't give a damn about her next of kin, but even at the moment, she knew some other unfortunate family would be getting a visit exactly like the one she was suffering through to tell them someone they loved was dead. It wasn't their fault their loved one was a whore who dated married men.

Could she even do this? There was a slim chance she would know who the woman was, anyway. She knew it wouldn't be any of her friends or fellow teachers. They wouldn't do that to her. That left his business acquaintances.

"I don't know how much help I can be. I didn't know any of Kevin's associates except a few I met at the holiday party a few weeks ago."

"Still, it would be helpful if you'd try. Is there someone you can call to go with you?"

She thought of her best friend, Lucy, but dismissed the idea immediately. They'd been arguing. Lucy was angry at Cali for letting Kevin treat her so badly. She wouldn't be able to hold her tongue, and as angry as she would no doubt be one day at Kevin for cheating on her, at that minute, all Cali wanted to do was cry for his sudden loss.

"No. I'll go alone. Let me change."

Cali moved on autopilot, refusing to let the news sink in deep enough to hurt her. She went through the motions of putting on a worn pair of jeans and a sweater. She slipped on a pair of flats and pulled her long, thick black hair back in a ponytail. Out of habit, she reached for her makeup. Kevin had made sure she always looked her best when she left the house. As she looked at the pale version of her disheveled self in the large mirror, the reality started to sink in.

Kevin was gone. He would never again be there to even notice how she looked. Emotions raged through her brain—conflicting and confusing emotions she knew she needed more than a few minutes to examine. She forced them down deep, vowing to get through the next few hours, then she could collapse later when she was alone again.

The drive to the county morgue was thankfully short. With each minute that passed, she felt more numb. She was conscious enough to suspect she was in shock, but she was helpless to change it. She let herself be led by the two kind officers through a darkened building, quiet at five in the morning. They stopped outside a room with a plaque on the outer door labeling it as the County Morgue.

Officer Jackson sensed her fear and wrapped his arm

around her supportively. "We'll be there with you Mrs. Bennett. The coroner will pull back the sheet covering just the face of the victim long enough to see if you can identify her."

She didn't answer. It didn't seem like she needed to. He led her through the double doors, across the large, clinical room to a small alcove sectioned off by hanging draped partitions like you'd see at an emergency room. Her eyes flew to the two long tables sitting side by side, both covered with white sheets.

Cali felt as if she were leaving her body, levitating above the surreal spectacle. It was as if she were living this scene through someone else's eyes. It seemed her brain knew it was the only way she could get through.

The three men in the room let her stand rooted to her spot until she finally looked up into the kind eyes of the elderly man she assumed was the coroner. He smiled a mourning smile he must have perfected over his decades in his grizzly job.

"Mrs. Bennett, I'm sorry for your loss. This has to be very hard for you. I do appreciate you coming down here tonight to try to help us identify the second victim in your husband's car. I'm going to warn you. There was some obvious damage done in the accident. This won't be easy. I'll pull back the sheet covering the woman..."

Cali cut him off. "I want to see Kevin first."

"I don't think that's a good idea, Mrs. Bennett. I'm sure you'd rather remember your husband as he was alive. Not here tonight."

"I want to see Kevin. I *need* to see Kevin. I won't believe it was him until I do."

The three men shared a concerned glance before the doctor walked around to the other body. Cali felt her feet move like lead to stand next to the doctor. She took a deep breath as he pulled the sheet back from the face of the dead body below. That brief second seemed to last a lifetime. She wasn't sure what she hoped at that moment. Life with Kevin had been difficult, but there was a small part of her that still loved him.

There was no doubt. The body was that of her husband. She could see multiple deep cuts and abrasions, and it was clear the doctor had attempted to clean him up at least a little. He was so white... chalky. She reached to touch him, but the doctor stopped her.

"You won't want to do that, Mrs. Bennett. His body is already getting cold. It's best if you remember him as he was."

She bent to his guidance, unable to rally enough emotion to do anything but follow directions. A single tear tracked down her cheek as the sheet was replaced over his face. It felt so final.

The doctor looped his arm through her own, leading her slowly around to the second covered body in the room. Cali had almost forgotten about this part.

"Again, I'm sorry to make you go through this after all you've already experienced. This victim has a bit more damage than your husband."

For the first thirty seconds after the sheet was pulled back, Cali had to fight back the urge to puke. The head of the dead woman on the table was crushed in several places, making it impossible to make out her facial features. Her question flew out, unguarded.

"She must not have been wearing her seatbelt?"

When none of the men answered her, she looked up, locking eyes with the doctor. "She wasn't wearing a seatbelt."

Cali's sixth sense picked up on the doctor's hesitation. "What aren't you telling me?" she probed.

The doctor hedged. "You don't want to know the gory details..."

"Tell me everything. I deserve to know the truth," she urged.

The three men in the room exchanged worried glances. Kevin was dead. Didn't they realize there couldn't be worse news than that?

The doctor finally nodded before choosing his words carefully, his answer clinical. "Based on the evidence at the scene, we believe this woman had your husband's penis in her mouth at the time of impact. His organ was severed completely, and her head was crushed between the steering wheel, the airbag, and your husband."

Calista's legs collapsed from under her. The officers were not fast enough to catch her before she slammed her head against the metal of the stainless-steel examination table holding the woman's body—the woman who had bitten Kevin's cock off his body.

Finally... emotions coursed through her body. Many conflicting emotions, but the most prevalent was rage—pure, unadulterated fury. It manifested itself in manic laughter. The officers attempted to lift her to her feet, but she slapped their hands away. She sat on the cold concrete floor of the darkened morgue, laughing and sobbing in equal measure. Surely, this was what a nervous breakdown felt like.

To their credit, the men stepped back, letting her expend her rage until she had no more tears. Officer Jackson held out several tissues for her as Officer Stanton helped her to her feet. They were being so kind, yet she felt infuriated they had put her in this position. It was wrong of them to ask her to identify the woman who had severed Kevin's cock. Strange thoughts flicked through one's brain in times of stress, and Cali wondered that surely, there had to be some unspoken etiquette rule about this.

A sudden need to be as far away as possible from this room of death consumed her. She needed to think. She started to step away, but the doctor had lowered the sheet to display more of the woman. Cali avoided looking at the mangled face but focused on the shoulder length sandy blond hair with salon highlights. Nothing remarkable. The body wore a gold necklace, again nondescript.

It was only when the doctor pulled the body's left hand from under the sheet to hold it up for Cali's examination that the first flare of recognition stirred. In her precarious state, it didn't come to her immediately. A niggling memory floated through her brain, trying to take hold. The long, manicured fingernails were not unusual. It was the wedding ring. The home-wrecker was married too. Somewhere, a husband slept in their bed not knowing his wife had died a few hours ago with another man's cock in her mouth. A wave of empathy for the unknown man invaded. Only she could know what he would soon face.

It took several long minutes before it came to her. She forced her brain to focus long enough to remember seeing that huge square cut ring with dozens of surrounding baguettes set in white gold. She had admired it at the time while thinking the shrew wearing it didn't deserve it. She snorted a laugh as she realized maybe the bitch had gotten exactly what she deserved.

Cali looked at the officer across the body from her. Their eyes locked before she answered his questioning gaze.

"Her name was Veronica Mikos. Her husband is a lawyer at the same law firm where my husband worked. His name is Nicholas Mikos."

CHAPTER 4

"*N*ick. Did you hear what I said?" Nick had been lost in thought, staring out the kitchen window into his backyard. The fresh snow cover had a way of hiding the ugly, frozen ground. He wished it could hide the ugly reality of the last three days. He reluctantly turned his attention to his older sister, standing at his kitchen island.

"I'm gonna wrap up some of these leftovers and put them in the freezer. There's no way you and Andi are going to be able to work through these before they go bad, and it'll be good for you to have some meals you can pull out later."

It was just like Natalie to be taking charge. He knew she was coping, trying to help her baby brother in any way she could. What else could she do to help? Veronica, his wife and the mother of his only child was dead. That alone would be hard to deal with. It was the humiliating way she had died that made the already bad situation that much worse.

Nick had seen the pity in the eyes of his friends and neighbors at the closed-casket funeral this morning. The local newspaper had done a stellar job with their investigation into the fatal car accident. He didn't blame the media.

Not really. Two married people killed while sneaking around behind their spouse's backs—it was a salacious story.

Nick had barely slept since the police came to the house Friday morning. He'd been trying to get Andi ready for school so he could drop her off on his way to the office.

Roni had told him she needed to go to New York to visit her sister whose marriage was crumbling. Only when his sister-in-law had shown up with her husband in tow for the funeral did Nick know the excuse had been completely fabricated. Veronica's lie had set things in motion to allow his wife the opportunity to die in the car with that prick, Kevin Bennett. The fact she had cheated on him was bad enough, but that it was with the pretentious asshole Roni knew he hated made it hurt that much worse. So far, the only consolation he had received was that at least the bastard had paid with his life.

Nick mourned for his lost wife—his lost marriage. Even more, he mourned for his daughter's lost mother. No seven-year-old should have to lose a parent. It wasn't right. Still, as he moved to the doorway to the dining room, he watched Andi playing a board game with her grandma. Only her simple black dress gave away her recent loss. He didn't think his daughter really understood what was happening around her, and for that, he was grateful. There would be plenty of time for her to come to terms with their loss.

She looked up then, smiling a comforting smile that seemed beyond her young years. Damn, he loved that little girl. She was all he had left of Roni now. As Andi returned to the spirited game, oblivious to his pain, Nick remembered the first time he had set eyes on her.

She had been a few weeks old by the time he met his daughter. He had dated Roni for a few months the year before, breaking things off when he had seen how manipulative she could be. When she'd shown up on his doorstep with a baby who looked exactly like him, his heart melted on the spot. Andi had his olive skin and black hair. She'd opened her eyes and stared directly into his soul just before the month-old baby broke out into the most beautiful smile he had ever seen. He knew at that moment his life would never be the same.

They had married just a few weeks later. Nick had a lot of regrets about his tumultuous relationship with his dead wife, but he'd never regret she gave him Andrea. She was perfect. A wave of panic invaded as Nick worried for the hundredth time how he was going to manage raising Andi on his own. Veronica may have never won the mother-of-the-year award, but she was at least there to do what needed to be done. Even after Andi was in school, Roni had elected not to work. At Nick's insistence, she had shuffled Andi to gymnastics and dance lessons over the last few years. Nick mentally added finding a nanny for his daughter to his growing to-do list.

"Have you thought about what you're going to do next?" His sister had come up beside him to look at the handful of remaining close friends and family members milling about. Part of him wanted to scream at everyone to get the hell out so he could be alone and think. The other part of him was terrified to be alone in the house with just Andi. He knew that would be when it would really hit him Roni was gone.

He finally answered his sister, "Not really. I've taken the next two weeks off to try to get my head on straight and figure out what I'm gonna do."

"I wish I could stay to help longer, but I can only stay a couple more days."

"It's okay, Nat. I know you can't be away from the kids and the restaurant forever."

"They'll be okay without me for a few days. I'm gonna make you an offer, but I don't want you to be pissed at me."

He heard the hesitancy in her voice and turned to look down into her eyes before she continued. "I can't stay, but I'm happy to take Andi home with me." Nick immediately started to interrupt, but she held her fingers to his lips to shush him. "Not forever. Just until you have time to figure out what you want to do."

There was no way he was gonna let his little girl leave. "I appreciate the offer, Nat and I know you mean well, but Andi belongs here with me. I'll figure something out."

The laughter of his daughter and mother as they played the game seemed out of place in the melancholy room. Brother and sister watched the two people they both loved so much having fun.

"I'd leave mom here if I thought she would be a help, but she's been getting worse. I'm afraid leaving her here would do more harm than good for you."

"I've noticed she's getting more forgetful. I hate how fast the Alzheimer's is progressing."

"Don't worry about that right now. You have enough shit on your plate. I can handle mom."

"Thanks, Nat. I don't think I can deal with anything more right now."

"I get that. If I didn't have my hands full with the kids and the restaurant, I'd stay. You know that, right?"

"I do, but truthfully, I need some time alone to sort through everything that's happened."

"I understand. Just promise me you'll call if you need to talk, okay?"

"I will."

Several hours later, the house was quiet. The mourners had left, and his mom and sister had gone upstairs to give Andi her bath and get her settled in for the night. Nick sat alone for the first time since receiving the news of his wife's death. His wife's betrayal. He downed his third bourbon, enjoying the burn trailing down his throat to his sour stomach. He enjoyed the rush of the alcohol. It would be so easy to lose himself in self-pity. The only thing stopping him was the thought of the beautiful daughter sleeping one story above him.

Instead of grabbing for the bourbon bottle, Nick pushed to his feet. He took the stairs in twos, rushing up to open the door to his daughter's princess themed bedroom. The small nightlight illuminated the room. It gave him enough light to see her angelic face as he stood over her. He was comforted by the even rise and fall of her chest in sleep, relieved she didn't seem upset by the fact her mother wasn't there like normal.

Nick pulled the wooden rocking chair over from the corner. He'd spent countless hours rocking his daughter in that chair, reading her bedtime stories. Tonight, he would sleep in it, rocking as he kept watch over her until exhaustion finally allowed him to slip into a fitful sleep.

Cali was exhausted. She shouldn't be. It was only four in the afternoon, but today had been hard. It was her first day back in the classroom since Kevin's accident. The school had given her three weeks off to take care of things and to mourn her husband's sudden death. She knew she should be grateful for the time off, but after struggling to hold her emotions in check all day, she wondered if she was ready to go back to work. On the one hand, it was good to have something routine to get her mind off all she'd been through. On the other hand, the pitiful looks she got from her peers as she passed them in the hallway kept her locked in the hell Kevin had thrown her into.

She had spent much of the last three weeks curled up in a ball, in the middle of their king-sized bed. She felt like a schizophrenic, fighting widely fluctuating mood swings. One minute, she would be fine, then she'd remember having to stand in the morgue to identify the woman who had bitten her husband's dick off and anger would consume her. Rage was becoming a frequent companion, and she hated it.

Then there were the times she would remember Kevin as he was when they'd met, the Kevin she had fallen in love with. But it was the tyrant who would hurt her with his rough sexual domination that consumed her dreams. She often awoke in a cold sweat, unable to get back to sleep. Only now were the last of the bruises finally fading.

She took a nap when she got home and woke somewhat rested. Her cell phone rang with a call from her dad. She let it roll to voicemail. He'd come to the funeral, of course. He had even tried to convince her to move back to Baltimore for a while, but she knew there would be no peace in her childhood home. She would just be trading in one set of bad memories for another.

Things hadn't been the same with her family for years. Family trauma had torn them apart while she was still in her teens. She had been relieved to leave for college to escape the constant strain and bickering. She was halfway through her freshman year when her mom had died of a heart attack. Her dad had never been the same since. Now, years later, things were as strained as ever.

Her phone rang again. This time it was her best friend, Lucy. She picked up at the last minute. "Hey."

"So how did the first day back at work go?"

"As you'd expect. Hard and long. Emotional, yet good to get out of the house. Basically, as confusing as ever."

"You won't be confused forever, Cal. Sooner or later,

you'll only remember the bad shit he did, and you'll be able to leave him in your dust."

"If you called just to bash Kevin, I'll hang up now. I know you hated him, but he was my husband."

"He was your abuser, Cali. You were brainwashed."

"Gotta go. Talk to you..."

"Fine. I'll stop talking about him. I actually called to see if you've talked to your dad today."

"No, but he tried to call a few minutes ago. I let it roll to voicemail."

"Well, I ran into him at the grocery store today. He looked like shit."

"I'm sorry for that, but I sort of have my plate full right now."

"I'm just saying. Maybe you two could help each other. He acted like guilt is eating him alive over how your mom died, and now, he feels so bad for you. It was weird. He kept saying how sad it was that you wouldn't be able to have the family you deserved."

A pang of sadness contracted her heart. She couldn't go there.

"Well, it wasn't for lack of trying on Kevin's part."

Her best friend snorted, but to her credit, didn't take the opportunity to disparage Kevin again. "I'm just saying you might want to call your dad."

"Fine. I'll think about it."

"Okay, I gotta go. Love you, kiddo."

"Later. Thanks for calling, Luc."

Cali had been pacing around the massive house as she spoke to her friend. Not for the first time since Kevin died did she ponder what she should do with the big house. They had bought it with a sizable monetary gift from Kevin's parents for their wedding. It was meant to be the home they would raise the kids that would never be. She knew she needed to sell the house and move, but she had no idea where. She had decided it was best to wait a few months before she made any major decisions.

Every night during the three weeks since he'd died, Cali had nervously paced the house. In all that time, she'd been avoiding her husband's home office. In part, because she'd rarely been in that particular room, but more importantly because the few times she had been there were not particularly fond memories.

She had received her first punishment spanking bent over the large wooden desk where her husband liked to work. As angry as she'd been at him, even now, she knew she had deserved that particular punishment. She had crashed her car into a parked van while texting in the parking lot at the mall. It had caused over ten thousand dollars in damages, and their insurance premium had gone up.

As she stood in the entry to the room, looking at that desk, she knew that had been the day her marriage had changed forever. It was that fateful day she'd discovered her husband was a sadist who enjoyed punishing his wife. She had also discovered, in spite of the pain and how much she hated the loss of control, there was a hidden part of her that responded to Kevin's domination. Even now, over a year later, she still didn't understand how her body could react the way it had under his domination. She'd love to blame Kevin for being abusive as Lucy insisted, but only Cali knew he had unlocked a submissive part of her she'd worked hard to keep hidden deep inside. How much easier would life have been if she'd told him to fuck off that fateful night?

Cali sat in the executive chair behind the desk, looking through the open files and loose papers her husband had left behind. The mail had been piling up on the front entry table. She'd paid a few of the bills she knew she needed to take care of but also knew there was a plethora of paperwork she needed to sort through here in his office.

She dreaded it.

Cali forced herself to start by opening the top drawer but found nothing out of the norm. She discovered his handgun in the second drawer down, a box of ammunition next to it. Cali avoided touching the weapon, leaving it where it was. It was what she found deeper in the drawer that drew her attention. She picked up the small external drive and wondered what kind of information Kevin had stored on it.

His personal laptop sat on top of the desk. She slid her fingers across the mousepad, waking it up. It was plugged into power and fully charged. She didn't have his password and knew the chances of guessing were slim to none. She plugged the hard drive into the USB port, but nothing happened. She continued rifling through the desk to see what else she could find. As she opened the center top drawer, a post-it note with a strange code was on top.

Could it be that easy?

Cali was amazed when the password unlocked the laptop. It wasn't like Kevin to be so careless with sensitive information. Still, she took a few minutes to poke around. There were hundreds of files and directories devoted to clients and some for their personal finances. She'd have to spend time looking through them later.

It was the file marked as 'cell phone backup' that caught her eye. Kevin's cell had been destroyed in the accident. She'd regretted that because she was sure there were names and addresses in his phone she needed to send out thank-yous to after the funeral. Cali poked around through the directories until she found his contact list.

It was when she saw "Roni," her curiosity turned to anger. The number was local. There was no last name, but she knew. Unable to stop herself, she clicked through the backup, looking through saved text messages and emails until she hit the jackpot.

She read for over two hours—there were that many messages between the lovers. She had naively thought her husband had been attracted to Veronica at the party back in January. What a fool she'd been. The emails went back at least six months before that. Love emails. Sexting. Photos. Texts of where to meet. Each one cut her wounds open just a bit wider—a bit deeper.

The emails where they discussed how clueless both Nick and Cali were hurt the worst. They had ridiculed their spouses often for being so naive and trusting. After all the tears she had shed for Kevin, these personal messages felt like his final betrayal. For the first time, she truly hated him. She hoped they were happily rotting in hell together.

A wave of nausea hit, and Cali found herself puking up her dinner into the nearby trashcan. As she was throwing up, a sharp pain cramped, and she found herself running to the bathroom. She finished being sick for the second time before sitting.

The sight of the deep red blood in her underwear shouldn't have surprised her. She had intellectually known there was no possibility of being pregnant. She had been a week late starting her period, and there was a small part of her that had begun to wonder if she might have a baby growing inside her after all. Her brain knew this was for the best, but finding the evidence of Kevin's long-time infidelity combined with the arrival of her period was the final straw.

Cali ripped the clothes off her body as fast as she could. She started the shower, getting in while the water was ice cold, welcoming the shocking temperature. The harshness woke her from the veil of naivety she had been living under. As the water warmed and finally turned to steaming hot, Cali welcomed the pain of the burn where the water met skin.

She allowed the bite of heat to punish her for her stupidity. She sat on the floor of the shower, hugging her knees to her chest, rocking until the water began to cool.

Cali relocated to the bedroom, stopping only to grab a bottle of vodka and orange juice. For the next hour, she drank enough alcohol to dull the pain. When it wasn't enough, she took a pair of scissors to their walk-in closet and shredded several of Kevin's most expensive suits and ties. It felt good to see the evidence of her fury piled in the center of the oversized closet. She curled up in the middle of the pile.

She felt utterly alone. No one understood what she was going through. Not really. Everyone tried to be nice, but her in-laws had deserted her. It was as if they somehow held her responsible for the loss of their son. She was estranged from her dad. Her mom was gone. Lucy tried to help but only knew how to hate Kevin.

It was at that moment she thought of Nicholas Mikos. She hadn't thought of him since the funeral. She wondered what Nick was doing right that minute. How was he dealing with his wife's betrayal? At least he had his daughter to cling to. A new regret that she wasn't pregnant invaded. It would have been nice to have a blessed occasion like a baby to wipe away some of her sorrows.

The vodka had done its job. Cali drifted in and out of a fitful sleep while curled up on the floor of the closet. It was after midnight when she found herself awake again, unable to get back to sleep. She had only a long, lonely night to look forward to.

Cali wasn't sure of her plan until she found herself sitting behind Kevin's large desk again. She moved on autopilot as she looked up Nicholas Mikos in her husband's contact list. It wasn't surprising to find it there, they had worked together after all. She had had just enough vodka to dull her decision-making ability.

It rang several times before a masculine voice answered. "Hello?"

What the hell was she doing? She was about to hang up when he spoke again. "Who's there? If this is another reporter looking for a story, fuck off."

He sounded so angry. He deserved to be angry. So did she.

"Nick?" Her voice was barely a whisper, but he heard.

"Cali?"

She held her breath. Unsure if she should answer.

He persisted "Cali? Is that you?"

"Yes." She'd been so angry before the call. Why were tears prickling her eyes at the sound of his voice?

He sighed. "I'm glad you called. I've wanted to call you a few times but didn't have your number. And I didn't know... well... you know."

"Unfortunately, I do know." They let a long awkward silence stretch out.

He broke the quiet. "I've been worried about you. How are you?"

"Probably about the same as you."

"That bad, eh?" He tried to laugh it off. It sounded strained. They fell into silence again.

"I'm sorry. I don't know why I called. I'll let you go." Cali felt foolish for calling.

"Please. Don't go." She heard a familiar desperation in his voice.

"What do you want me to say, Nick? Anything we talk about is only going to make us feel worse."

"I don't think so. I hate it, but you're the only person who could possibly understand what it's like. You're a beautiful, smart woman. You didn't deserve this to happen to you, Cali. I want you to know that."

The tears she had been holding back fell fast. She hadn't

thought he could say anything to make her feel better, but she'd been wrong. He had somehow known exactly what she'd needed to hear.

"Thank you for saying that," she answered through her tears. "You certainly didn't deserve this either. No one knows what to say, you know? They either avoid me or try to cheer me up. They don't know that maybe I need to wallow for a while, you know?"

"Boy, do I ever. I finally went into the office today, and it was brutal."

"I went back to school today, too. Brutal is the perfect word."

"Is that why you called?"

Cali debated lying, but then she'd be doing to him what his wife had done. As ugly as the truth was, he deserved to hear it. "No. Not really."

"Well, I'm glad you did."

"I bet you wouldn't be if you'd found what I found tonight."

He hesitated. He must have been deciding if he wanted her to continue. "Maybe you should tell me and let me be the judge of that."

"There'll be no unhearing the words once they're said," she tried to warn him.

"Just like there will be no bringing them back."

"Would you want to even if you could?" Cali asked curiously.

She started to wonder if the call had dropped. He finally answered. "Would it make me a monster if I said no?"

"No, it makes you human. I might have said yes yesterday, but not tonight. Tonight, I hope they're rotting in hell."

Nick whistled the surprised kind of whistle. "That doesn't sound good. Maybe you're right. Maybe I don't want to know." He hesitated. "Like it or not, I need to know. I'm tired of the secrets—of the lies. I found a couple credit cards I didn't know about last week. A nice little fifteen-thousand-dollar fuck-you courtesy of my wife from her grave."

"Don't scare me. I haven't even braved the finance crap yet." She hoped she didn't have more surprises waiting for her there. "I've just been paying a few bills I know about. I'm dreading it. I know I'll have to tackle it soon."

"So if not finances, what did you find?"

"You're sure?"

"Positive."

She took a deep breath. "How long do you think they were seeing each other?"

He answered quickly. "Well since they met at the holiday..." his voice trailed off. He never finished his thought.

"Try a bit longer."

"Goddamn her. How do you know?"

"I finally got logged onto his personal laptop. He had a backup file of his phone. It was how I got to his contact list. Do you have her cell phone? If you do, you could find it all too."

"No. I never found her phone. I assumed she had it with her, and it was destroyed in the accident."

"How much do you want to know?"

"I want it all. The truth for once."

"I found stuff going back at least six months. I'm not sure how it started, but I found emails, texts, photos... you name it. They communicated almost daily." She had expected him to be angry. She hadn't expected silence.

"Nick? Are you still there?" When he didn't reply, she tried again. "I'm so sorry. I should never have told you."

"You did the right thing, Cali." She heard the barely contained rage in his voice. "I just don't know if I can believe it. I mean... not that you... I'd just like to think I would have noticed something like that, you know?"

It was Cali's turn to get angry. "You better not be insinuating I'm lying to you. I'm not Veronica. Not every woman is a lying bitch."

He sighed. "I wasn't trying to imply you were lying. It's just so... I didn't think it could get any worse. I was wrong."

"Honestly, as much as I hurt now, I think this will help me get over him sooner. Kevin was a bit like Jekyll and Hyde. He could be so charming when he wanted to be. The next minute he could call me every condescending name he could think of while..." She cut herself off. She wasn't ready to share how abusive Kevin could get.

"While he what, Cali?"

"Nothing. It's not important now. I'm sorry if this news hurt you, but I just know if you'd found this evidence, I would have wanted you to share it with me, you know? I'm so tired of his lies."

"Cali, would you consider having dinner with me some time? Before you think I'm coming on to you or something, I'm not. I'd just like to talk with you more. I think we could help each other through some of the shit, you know? Maybe you could bring his laptop along and let me see some of the messages?"

"I don't think that's a good idea, Nick."

"Which part? Dinner or the laptop?"

"Both."

"Please. Friday night. I can have Andi sleepover at her best friend's house."

"Let me think about it, okay?"

"Okay. Is this your cell phone you called from?"

"Yes."

"Then we'll talk later in the week. Think about it, Cali. It would mean a lot to me."

"Goodnight, Nick."

"Goodnight, Cali. Try to get some sleep."

CHAPTER 5

"*W*ould you like another drink, sir?" The portly
bartender reached to take away his empty
rock glass. Nick wanted another to calm his nerves.

"Not yet. I'll wait for my companion to join me first,
thanks."

He'd arrived early at the Greek restaurant in his old
haunting ground near Georgetown. He'd been relieved when
Cali had texted him the night before, agreeing to meet for
dinner. He'd begun to worry she wouldn't feel up to it. Not
that he blamed her. A part of him dreaded learning more
about how Veronica had made a fool out of him, but he'd
begun to think of tonight as the figurative ripping off of the
band-aid. It may hurt worse for a bit, but it would help heal
the wounds she'd inflicted faster.

That was the plan, anyway.

Calista had asked him to pick a place to meet. He'd
chosen Georgio's for two reasons. One, Veronica had hated
Greek food and refused to eat there. More importantly, it
would be easier for the two of them to disappear into the sea
of people on a Friday night in a college neighborhood. He

didn't want to risk meeting anywhere near either of their homes on the off chance they might be seen by someone either of them knew.

"Nick?"

He'd been lost in thought and missed her arrival. Nick swung around to greet her. He'd forgotten how beautiful she was with her silky black hair, amber-brown eyes, olive skin, and hourglass figure. He couldn't believe what a stupid fuck Kevin Bennett had been to cheat on someone like Cali.

Their eyes locked as they silently sized each other up. The surrounding candlelight reflected off the tears that glistened in her eyes. She looked as fragile as he'd been feeling the last four weeks. It was odd a strength he hadn't felt minutes before surged through him, urging Nick to protect the woman standing before him from any more harm.

A tear spilled over and trickled down her cheek. He longed to reach out and swipe it away. Her eyes widened in surprise when he gently cupped her face. It gave her the courage to rush into his arms, hugging him with all her strength.

A cocktail of emotions rushed Nicholas as he held her. It only got worse as her tears turned to sobs. He should have picked a more private place to meet. Restaurant patrons were watching them. Nick stroked her long, black hair as he rocked her gently in his arms.

"Shhh, Cali. It may not feel like it, but it's gonna be okay."

He took the handkerchief out he had been clairvoyant enough to bring along. After she'd calmed, he let her dry her eyes before he took her by her elbow and escorted her toward the restaurant portion of the establishment. He'd made reservations, and they were ushered to a private booth at the back of the dimly lit restaurant. Once seated, an awkward silence stretched between them. Nick tried to put her at ease.

"Thanks again for calling me, Cali. I think you're the first person I've talked to since... the accident... who understands what I'm going through."

He saw her exhale as if she'd been holding her breath. "I'm relieved. I wasn't sure if you'd be angry for... well... you know."

"I may be angry about a lot of things, Cali, but I promise you, you're the last person that anger is directed at. Unfortunately, the two people who deserve my hatred can't be here. I don't blame you for marrying an asshole."

Nick regretted the words as soon as they left his mouth. He may have hated Kevin Bennett, but Cali was still mourning her loss. She didn't need to be put in a position to defend him. Cali responded before he could apologize.

"I don't blame you for hating him. Most days I hate him too. I can't say I think of your wife kindly either." She tried to smile, but it came off more as a grimace.

Nick paused before admitting what he'd been struggling with.

"I've been trying to blame Kevin for corrupting her, but it isn't working. Deep down, I knew she wasn't happy anymore. I was never ambitious enough for Veronica. She was furious I wasn't made associate partner yet. I don't even think it was about the money, but more about the prestige. I've had a lot of time to reflect on it, and I think it was so important to her, she gave up on me and moved on to Kevin, knowing as a Bennett, he would certainly be a partner soon."

He watched for her reaction. She didn't look surprised.

"I wish I knew if he'd planned on leaving me for her. He was furious..." She stopped abruptly as she weighed her next words. "It's not important now, I guess."

He pressed her. "What could he possibly be angry at you about?"

"Let's just say you aren't the only one who disappointed their spouse."

"Well, then he was a bigger idiot than I gave him credit for."

After their waitress took their order and brought them their drinks and appetizer of flaming cheese, Nick broached the subject that had brought them together.

"Did you bring the laptop with the backup?"

Cali hesitated. "You're sure? I've read more. Trust me when I say, it's gonna hurt to read it."

"I don't have a choice. I need to know, so I can move on."

Cali reached into her purse and pulled out a small USB thumb drive. She slowly pushed it across the table between them. Nick extended his hand, and for a few brief seconds, their fingers brushed.

He despised the circumstances that brought them to this place and time together, but in that minute, he felt a bond with the fragile woman sitting across the table. Even if they never saw each other again after tonight, they would forever be intimately linked, having been put through the same ordeal by their spouses. Kevin and Veronica had set things in motion, and Nick and Cali were going along for the ride.

Calista's words brought him back to the present.

"There was too much to read here in the restaurant, and anyway, you'll want to read it when you're alone."

"I'll have to read it when Andi is gone then."

"How is your daughter doing with her loss?" Her look of concern was genuine.

"Honestly, Andi is doing remarkably well. I'm not sure if you picked up on it in our short time together at the holiday party, but Roni didn't enjoy being a mother. Not really. Andrea was less dependent on her mom than I realized."

"Did you make her get pregnant?" Calista's face turned a

bright red. "I'm so sorry. That was a rude question. It's none of my business."

"Don't worry about hurting my feelings, Cali," Nick tried to put her mind at ease. "You can ask me anything, and while I was definitely thrilled when we had Andrea, it was a shock. See, Roni and I had broken up sometime before. She showed up on my doorstep when Andi was a few weeks old with a sob story about not being able to abort my baby because she was still in love with me. Even now, knowing how things turned out, I don't regret it. Roni and I may have had our problems, but making Andrea was the one thing we did right."

"You're lucky to have her. The house is so empty now."

"Does your family live nearby? Are they helping out?"

A new sadness moved into Cali's eyes. "I grew up in Baltimore. My parents moved over from Greece a few years before I was born. They opened a restaurant in Greektown, so I grew up working there. I'd always planned on sticking with the family business, but then... well... my parents and I were close until I was in high school." She paused as if she was figuring out what she wanted to share. "Then we hit kind of a rough patch and grew apart. I got a great scholarship and left for college. I hoped the time apart would help us heal, but mom died suddenly when I was a freshman in college. Dad's been a hot mess ever since. We've remained pretty estranged. He came to Kevin's funeral, but I don't expect to hear from him again anytime soon."

"I'm sorry you don't have a support system."

"My best friend, Lucy, has been a big help. How about you? Other than Andi that is."

"I grew up in a suburb of Detroit. As you may have guessed with the last name Mikos, my family is from Greece as well although we've been in the States a few more generations than your family. I have an older sister, then I came along many years later as their 'oops.' Dad died of a heart attack about ten years ago and my sister, Natalie, and I have the joy of watching our mother sinking deeper into the throes of early onset Alzheimer's."

"I'm so sorry. That must be so hard to watch your mom changing like that."

"Thanks, and yes, it is. They came for the funeral, of course. Natalie was a big help, but she couldn't stay long. She has her own family, and they own a restaurant like your dad. Mom is too far gone to be able to help. I honestly don't know what I'm going to do. I'll be able to stay home for the next few weeks, but I'm sure George Bennett is going to want me back on the road meeting clients again soon. I can tell he's shaken up by his son's death, but he's managed to keep going into the office. I talked to him this afternoon. I couldn't help but get the feeling he blames me somehow for Kevin's death."

"I wouldn't put it past him. Kevin's family has pretty much dropped off the face of the earth since the funeral."

A strained silence stretched between them as the waitress delivered their entrees and refilled drinks. After she left, Cali asked, "How long have you worked at BB&M?"

"Since I passed the bar, just over eight years. Maybe having Bennett blame me is for the best. I haven't been happy there for a long time. I'm going to have to look for a job where I can be at home every night. I've tried hiring a nanny. I've called around town to several of the services. They've sent me dozens of resumes, and I've even met with a few ladies, but I just can't find anyone I would feel comfortable leaving Andi with for several days at a time, you know?"

"I hadn't thought of that. It's going to be hard for you. Kevin would be gone for days at a time." Their eyes met. He knew what she was going to say before she spoke. "Looking back, I wonder how many of those nights I thought he was away on business were actually spent with Veronica when you were out of town?"

A renewed wave of rage coursed through Nick at the thought of Roni meeting Kevin. Who had been watching Andi at the time? Had she left Andi home in bed alone to meet her lover? Had she snuck the bastard into their home and let him fuck her in their marital bed while their daughter slept down the hall? He hadn't spoken his suspicion, but when his eyes met Cali's, he could tell she knew what he'd been thinking.

"Unfortunately, as you'll find on the thumb drive, it was probably all the scenarios you just ran through your head."

"I'm so sorry, Cali."

"You're sorry? For what?"

"That my wife..."

"Stop. This isn't your fault any more than it's mine. Let the blame stay with them. They paid for it with their lives. I just want to put my life back together and figure out what I'm going to do next. I can't stay in the huge house alone, so I've already decided to sell it. I just don't know if I should stay in the area, move back to Baltimore, or move somewhere completely new and start all over again where no one looks at me with pity. Lucky for me, they need school teachers everywhere."

"I'm going through the same evaluation. I don't want to make Andi move schools and be away from her friends unless I have to though. Lucky for me, they need lawyers everywhere too."

They finished dinner, talking about much lighter topics. Only after they'd shared an order of Baklava and drank their strong after-dinner coffees did their conversation return to more personal topics.

"Thank you again for calling me the other night, Cali. I

know it wasn't easy for you. As hard as it is to talk about what happened, I still had a good time with you tonight."

"I'm glad I decided to come too. I'm not sure how you'll feel about this, but I'd like to offer to babysit Andi for you if you run into a pinch and don't have anyone else. I know she's never met me, but... well... I love kids, obviously, since I'm an elementary school teacher. I wasn't able to have kids of my own so being able to help you with Andi would actually be a treat for me."

Her offer came out of left field, Nick hadn't expected it. He hesitated long enough Cali shifted in her seat and looked embarrassed.

"Hey, never mind, I can tell you don't like the idea."

"I never said that. You just caught me off guard. Why would you offer to do something like that? You don't have any obligation to me, you know."

He saw the flash of anger in her amber eyes.

"I'm not offering out of obligation. I just thought we could help each other out. I'm lonely and have too much time on my hands, and until you find another job, you're gonna need someone to help with Andrea. If you don't want my help, that's fine. I understand."

"I'm sorry." He could see her pain. "I don't know what to say. I never expected the offer. Can you give me some time to think about it?"

"Sure, the offer won't expire. Just give me a call." The waitress arrived with their check, and she reached into her purse to pull out her wallet. Nick snatched it up.

"Oh no you don't. Dinner is on me, tonight. I asked you, remember?"

"That's not necessary, Nick. This wasn't a date. At least let me pay my half."

"Not on your life. This one is my treat. Maybe we can do this again sometime."

"Maybe." Her uneasiness shone through her eyes as she shifted in her seat. "Why don't you see how you feel after you read the USB drive?"

"Nothing I read on the drive is going to make me blame you, Calista. Nothing."

They settled the bill and left the restaurant together. Nick walked her to her car to make sure she made it safely. Only as their goodbyes were upon them did Nick realize just how much he didn't want the night to end. It had been the first night since the accident he'd felt alive again. He'd been going through the motions for a month.

Cali unlocked her door before turning back to Nick. "Thanks again for dinner, Nick. It was good to get out of the house."

"Thanks for calling and for the USB. Please... call me if you need anything, will you?"

"Sure. You too." Nick saw it in her eyes. She thought this was goodbye.

Just in case it was, Nick pulled her into his arms for a final hug. He felt a tremor rush through her body and knew she was cold in the late February chill. They embraced for several long seconds before Cali pulled out of their hug and rushed to sit behind the wheel. She gave a small wave as she pulled out into the snow-covered street. Nick stood and watched her drive away until she turned out of sight. He felt the USB drive in his pocket and knew he was going to be up all night reading.

CHAPTER 6

*C*alista shoved the stack of papers and lesson plans into her stylish leather briefcase. It wasn't that she was necessarily in a hurry to get home on another Friday night. Considering how long the weekends stretched out in the three months since Kevin's death, the only advantage of heading straight home from school was she could open the waiting bottle of wine sooner.

A fellow third-grade teacher, Bethany, called out as she passed her open classroom door. "Night, Cali. Hope you have a good weekend."

She stopped to poke her head in. "You too, Bethany. You and Jim have fun with your in-laws visiting."

"Very funny. I hope I'm still married when you see me on Monday."

"Me too. Just stay calm. They're leaving soon."

Cali headed out to the parking lot, thinking of how she'd love to get rid of her own in-laws. Since Kevin's death, they had barely checked in with her to see how she was doing, and when they had, each conversation had gotten more accusatory about what she'd done to push their son into the arms of another woman. Not once had they said they were sorry about how Kevin had treated her. Not once had they offered to help her sort out her finances. It had been up to her to figure out Kevin had neglected to purchase life insurance. It had been up to her to figure out how much debt they were in and how there was no way her teacher's salary alone was going to be able to dig herself out.

She wasn't looking forward to her appointment with a real estate agent the following day. It wasn't that she was emotionally attached to the house per se, but she wasn't prepared to deal with figuring out where she wanted to move yet. She was just grateful they had put close to fifty percent down on the house, with her in-law's help, of course. She would be fine financially once she got the equity out.

She was approaching her car when she looked beyond to see Nicholas Mikos walking toward her. He looked even more handsome than she remembered from their dinner a few months before. She stood rooted to her spot as their eyes locked. She hadn't expected him to seek her out in person.

"Cali, I'm sorry to startle you, but I was worried about you and... well... I wanted to talk to you."

"Nick, I didn't expect to see you here." Her brain was running at high speed, trying to think of the right thing to say.

"I understand, but you aren't taking my calls. I didn't want to come to the house, so I thought this would be the best place to approach you."

"I didn't take two of your calls, and that was after you ignored several of my texts first. I get it. I knew reading the stuff on the USB would change how you felt about everything."

"I'm sorry. I was a jerk not to respond. It just took some time to process everything."

"Hey, you don't need to explain it to me. And you don't

need to apologize. Just because my husband fucked your wife doesn't mean you owe me anything." Cali's anger had been lurking just under the surface for days. She had to hold it together during the week at school, but she'd found she needed the weekends to let it all out. Nick was catching the start of her weekend angst.

"Listen, I don't blame you for being pissed at me, I did kind of drop off the grid there for a while after reading everything. But that wasn't the only reason I didn't respond. Can we go somewhere and talk? Please."

"I don't think that's necessary."

"I do."

"Why?"

"Because I owe you answers, and I'm worried about you. I thought reading the messages Veronica had written to Kevin would be the hardest parts for me, but it wasn't. Reading how that asshole talked about you... treated you... it guts me, Cali. I didn't know how to handle talking to you about it." When Cali didn't respond, Nick added an invitation.

"Please, come to dinner with me tonight."

"I'm not hungry."

"Fine, drinks then."

"I'm not thirsty."

"Please. Give me a chance to explain."

Silence stretched between them as Cali weighed her options. She decided she could hear him out as long as alcohol was involved.

"Fine. Drinks. I hate Friday nights, anyway."

"Thanks. You want to leave your car here and ride with me?"

"No, I think it's best if I drive myself. I'll follow you."

Cali followed Nick to an Irish pub in downtown Falls Church. They parked in the back and went in the side door. Despite the bright spring sunlight, the pub was dimly lit.

They slid into a booth tucked away from the commotion around the large bar of Friday afternoon revelers.

Cali ordered a Cosmo in the hope of calming her ragged nerves triggered by Nick's unexpected appearance. She wasn't sure she wanted to hear what he had to say since reading all the private texts and emails on the USB.

After the waitress left, Cali broke their silence.

"So you got me here."

"Thanks again for coming. I have a couple of reasons for wanting to talk to you, and I'm trying to decide which I should start with. You..." Nick paused. Cali sensed his confusion. "You seem different, Cali. I'm worried about you."

"I'm sorry if I'm not living up to your expectations for how I'm supposed to grieve."

"Don't give me that shit. Don't forget who you're talking to. I'm not the enemy here, Calista."

Even Cali didn't understand where her anger was coming from, but she was fighting down the urge to scream.

"I'm sorry. I know you're not the enemy, Nick. I'm messed up, okay? I'm trying to get through one day at a time. Some days are better than others. Today is a bad day. I'm angry."

"At me?"

"At the world. I'm angry with Kevin for leaving me without life insurance and a boatload of debt. I'm angry with my in-laws for blaming me as if it were my fault I wasn't good enough for their son, he had to look outside our marriage. I'm furious at myself that I was actually afraid of losing him as if he were worthy of my love in the first place. And yes, I'm angry at you that the few times I reached out to you in the last few months because I needed to talk to someone who understood, you ignored me."

"I deserve that. I am sorry I haven't been there for you, but I'm here now, Cali."

"And why is that, exactly?"

"Because I wanted to confess to you in person."

That had her attention. "Confess to what?" She gulped down the last of her Cosmo and motioned to the passing waitress to bring her another.

"You realize you gave me Kevin's entire phone backup, right?"

The buzz of the strong cocktail was already dulling her reactions. It took her time to understand what he was implying.

"You read more than just the stuff between the two of them?"

"Yes."

"How much more?"

The waitress placed the next round and left before he answered.

"Everything. Every fucking word."

Memories she'd wanted to forget surfaced.

"That was an invasion of my privacy."

"Yes, and at first I felt guilty, but not anymore. The only one who should feel guilty is already dead. I just had to see your eyes when I ask you why? Why the hell did you stay with him? Why did you let him treat you like that? Why did you let him hurt you?"

He was fishing. Cali was pretty sure there was no proof of Kevin's physical abuse on his phone. Nick pressed her.

"He did hurt you, didn't he?"

"This is none of your business."

"You're right, but maybe I want it to be."

"That doesn't make sense."

"You once offered to help babysit Andi. That's the second reason I wanted to talk to you. I wanted to know if the offer still stood."

"You want me to babysit?"

"Yes. I've tried three nannies in eight weeks. One was worse than the next. I'll keep looking for a long-term solution, but I have to go to New York next week for two nights, and I'm really in a pinch. I get you're pissed at me, but I was hoping you'd help."

"What does me babysitting have to do with Kevin hurting me?"

"Nothing, I guess. I just knew if I saw you again, I'd need to confess I'd read everything. That I knew he was a bigger asshole than I even suspected."

"Yes, that he was."

"So, what do you say? Can you help me?"

"I don't know. Let me think about it."

"Okay. Maybe you could think about it over a burger? You should eat something if you're going to keep downing Cosmos at that rate."

"Thanks, Dad."

"Ouch. I know I'm a few years older than you, but that hurt."

Cali didn't stop her smile. "So, now we're even."

"Touché."

They manage to talk effortlessly for the next few hours while downing burgers and fries. Cali lost track of how many Cosmos she consumed, but they caught up to her when she stood to use the ladies room. By the time she got back to the booth, Nick had paid their bill and was holding her jacket for her. He waited until they were outside to steer her to his car. She tried to keep going to her own car, but Nick stole the keys out of her hand.

"Oh no, you don't. I'm not letting you drive in this condition. I stopped drinking a while ago." He held the passenger door open, waiting for her to sink into the sports car. One look at his face and she knew there would be no changing his mind. In truth, he was right. Once he was behind the wheel, he turned to her with a sad smile.

"I'd better drive carefully. We could really create a stir if we got in an accident riding in the same car."

Cali's guard was down. She blurted her first thought. "Well, I doubt we'll get in an accident unless you want me to give you a blowjob."

Nick had turned his attention to backing out, but he threw the car into park and stared at Cali. "What are you talking about?"

Cali's breath became short. Surely he knew? "Didn't you read the accident report from that night?"

"No. No one ever offered me a copy. It didn't seem important."

"I guess I'm not even sure if it's in there."

"What is?"

She was sobering up quickly. "Nothing. Never mind."

"Dammit, don't lie to me, Cali. What happened that night that I'm missing?"

Memories of identifying Veronica's smashed body had tears pooling.

"Did you know the police made me go to the morgue to identify the bodies? Kevin had ID on him, but they couldn't find any ID for Veronica."

"Wait. You saw her body?"

"Yes."

"We had a closed casket because..."

"You don't need to explain. I saw them both."

"Holy shit, I'm so sorry they made you do that. I had no idea."

"Seeing them both dead was horrible, but it was the callous way the coroner told me Veronica had bitten Kevin's cock off during the impact that shook me up. It was why she didn't have her seatbelt on."

For a minute, Cali wondered if he had even heard her. His first measurable reaction was a chuckle which quickly snowballed into manic laughter.

"Nick, are you okay?"

It took him a few minutes to get the reaction out of his system.

"That's priceless. Death by blowjob."

Nick finally got the car in motion, and Cali's stomach rolled as she processed the alcohol in her system. By the time they arrived at her house, she was regretting her last drink. She had her keys in her hand and turned to say goodbye, but Nick was already out of the car and opening her car door. He walked her to the front door, and when she had trouble with the lock, stepped in to help her in the darkness of the porch.

Once inside, she flicked on the lights in the foyer. Nick stepped in and glanced around before his eyes returned to hers. An awkward silence fell over them during their first private moment.

"Thanks again for coming tonight. Just let me know by Monday if you can watch Andi next Wednesday and Thursday night, and we can get the details together. If you need a ride to your car tomorrow, give me a call, and I'll drive you, okay?"

Cali knew he was waiting for her reply, but she was temporarily paralyzed by emotions she didn't want to examine too closely. When Nick leaned forward to place a platonic kiss on her cheek, she smelled the masculine scent of his aftershave. He allowed his cheek to rest against hers as he hugged her closer.

Adrenaline mixed with alcohol fueled her next fateful move. As Nick pulled away from her like the gentleman he was, Cali reached to hug his waist to her tightly. When he looked down into her eyes, she pushed to her tippy toes to close the distance between them and pressed her lips against his.

It started as a chaste kiss but didn't take long to escalate. Cali could taste the ale Nick had been drinking earlier as his tongue slipped between her lips. Her knees grew weak beneath her, and he strengthened the hold he had on her, ensuring she wouldn't topple over. He shuffled them backward until Cali pressed against the unforgiving front door at her back, Nick's solid body mashed against her.

By the time Nick pulled out of their kiss, they were both short of breath. Cali kept her eyes closed, afraid she'd see reproach in his gaze.

"Cali, baby, open your eyes."

When she did, he looked more in control than he had at any time since she'd met him. The desire she saw on his face confused her.

"I'm sorry. I shouldn't take advantage of you like this. You have enough shit on your plate to deal with without adding this to the pile." Figures he would apologize.

"What exactly is this?"

"A mistake, that's what it is."

"Ouch. So I'm a mistake?"

"Dammit, Cali. Stop putting words in my mouth. You know that's not what I meant."

"Do I? Listen, I get it. It's complicated, but I just thought..."

"Stop. It's the Cosmos talking."

"I'm not that drunk, Nick. I'm lonely. I know you could make me feel better."

"Maybe, but you'd only feel better for tonight. Tomorrow, you'd regret it."

"How do you know that?" Dare she finish her thought? "I've thought of you a lot since we had dinner. It's helped."

"Oh, Cali, I've thought of you too, but we're both so raw

right now. I don't want either of us to get hurt worse than we already are."

Her brain knew he was right, but her heart and the rest of her body weren't listening. Months of celibacy partnered with the feel of his growing erection through their clothes spurred her into action. Cali slid her hand between their bodies, caressing his hardened cock through his slacks. She watched his eyes smolder with desire as her stroking hand turned his manhood to rock.

"Please stay." She hated the desperation in her voice as she begged. "I don't want to be alone again tonight."

"Christ, Cali. You're not playing fair. I want you so bad, but I also feel like I'm supposed to be protecting you from anyone else hurting you, including me. Haven't you been hurt enough?"

"You'd never hurt me like Kevin, did." In her tipsy state, her thoughts were only of physical pain. "All the bruises are finally gone."

"That asshole! He left bruises?"

"Only during sex. He didn't really abuse me like hitting me or anything."

"What a fucking prince."

They were in a stare down. He was right. Cali wasn't playing fair, but she just couldn't stand the idea of being alone again tonight. She continued to stroke his erection through his clothes until she was sure she felt him beginning to tremble under the burden of holding back from acting on his desire. She suspected she would feel foolish in the light of day for acting so wanton, but she'd deal with that tomorrow. Tonight, she wanted Nick to bed her—to make love to her—to remind her she was worthy of his attention.

She knew the second Nick made up his mind to stay. The uncertainty left his eyes and was replaced with a possessive-ness that made her shiver. She was unprepared when he scooped her into his arms and turned toward the winding staircase that led to the upper floor bedrooms. At the top of the stairs, he finally spoke.

"Which way, Cali?"

"The double doors at the end of the hall."

Only after they were in the master bedroom did Cali second-guess her answer. Should they make love in her and Kevin's bed? The look of satisfaction in Nick's eyes as he realized where they were bothered Cali. Was he here for her or was he only interested in getting even with Kevin by fucking Cali in their marital bed?

She didn't have enough time to worry about it. Nick laid her head on the pillows before he stepped away from the bed to slowly undress. It was as if he were unwrapping a present for her. Her eyes darted back and forth between being consumed by the heat in his eyes and enjoying the gift of his athletic body as he took off each piece of clothing until he stood naked.

Cali let her eyes devour the rigid cock jutting out from his body. He was thicker than Kevin, and she admired the masculine package Nicholas Mikos presented. She began to feel apprehensive she wouldn't be able to match up to his expectations. Surely Roni was a better lover since Kevin sought her out. Would Nick be disappointed in her like Kevin always had been?

His words jarred her back to the present.

"Unbutton your shirt, Calista."

She moved in slow motion, following his direction until her blouse fell open to expose her baby-blue lace bra.

"Unzip your slacks. Push 'em down your legs."

Cali did as he asked, never taking her eyes away from his. She noticed his breath becoming more labored as she kicked her slacks to the floor. She was down to her bikini underwear.

Nick sat on the bed next to her. He reached out to stroke her bare stomach before lifting her to a sitting position long enough to divest her of her blouse and unhook her bra. He laid her back gently before he pulled her bra straps down her arms and tossed it to the floor.

His first touch to her breasts was tentative. She enjoyed watching his reaction as her nipples grew under his ministrations. For all of her flaws, she knew she had good cleavage. They were just a bit bigger than his large hands could handle. Nick got bolder, cupping and squeezing until her sensitive peaks stood at attention.

When Nick climbed onto the bed, he straddled her thighs, facing her and lunged forward to suck her tip into his hungry mouth. Cali was unaccustomed to the leisurely pace he was setting, particularly since he continued to make her the center of his attention. Cali lost herself in the sensation of his wet mouth sucking and nipping at her as he trailed kisses in the valley between her tits. She enjoyed running her fingers through his thick, black hair—holding him against her chest as if to subconsciously keep him from changing his mind.

He moved his lips lower, kissing his way to her belly button. He scooted down the bed so he could reach out and hook his fingers in the waistband of her panties. His eyes locked with her as he bared her pussy, pushing her legs open wide. Cali wanted to be embarrassed, but the look on his face wouldn't let her. The heat in his eyes made her feel beautiful —desired for the first time in a long time.

The first tentative swipes of his fingers through her slick folds pulled a groan from Cali. When he stopped to massage her clit, she felt her hips buck off the bed. His playful grin knocked the wind out of her—literally. She'd always known Nick was a handsome man, but as he knelt before her, preparing to claim her, she realized just how much she wanted this. If she were honest with herself, she'd been attracted to him the first night they'd met, yet she was certain they would have never acted on the attraction between them.

That was then, but this is now. Nick's warning about regretting their actions in the light of day flitted through her head. Was this just a one-night stand for him?

She didn't get to finish her analysis. Nick's mouth on her wet heat made it impossible to think of anything but the pleasure he was delivering. He refused to rush, spending long minutes licking... teasing... sucking... It was the slowest build up to a climax Cali could remember, but by the time he plunged two fingers deep inside her as he latched onto her clit, she crashed into the most exquisite orgasm of her life. She cried out as she bucked her hips off the bed, yet Nick's lips refused to leave her pussy until he had wrung every last drop of ecstasy from her.

Through narrowed eyelids, she watched him finally sit up. His face was wet with her juices. He looked quite pleased with himself as he grinned down at her playfully. Warning bells were going off. At that moment, the connection between them felt so strong, she worried after he left, there might be another empty hole left in her heart.

She didn't get to dwell on it because Nick was blanketing her, his elbows on either side of her head to hold himself above her. She felt the crown of his hard-on at the entrance to her core. She held her breath, waiting for him to slide inside. When it didn't come, she opened her eyes to find him waiting for her. He was holding on by a thread. He didn't say a word. He just peered into her eyes as if he could read her thoughts, and maybe he could because just as she was prepared to beg him to claim her, he pushed forward, piercing her channel. Her sheath was stretched as he filled her like she'd never been filled before. They groaned as he bottomed out against her cervix.

She could tell he was trying to be gentle, but she didn't want gentle. She needed him to claim her. She wanted him to erase the pain she'd been carrying for months. Her quiet, "Nick, please..." confused her because even she didn't know what she was asking for. Nick seemed to understand though because he pulled out of her body before ramming forward, again and again. Her cunt was so wet from her first orgasm, his shaft slid easily in and out in a naughty rhythm until she'd come for a second time.

"Dammit, Cali. I'm not going to last very long."

"It's okay. You've already taken care of me twice."

Their pounding coupling only lasted another minute before she watched the peak he'd been holding off wash over his handsome face. Nick pulled away from her to yank his cock out just in time to deposit his hot cum across her tummy. Until that very second, Cali hadn't even thought of protection. Because she and Kevin had been trying to conceive, she wasn't on birth control. She was grateful Nick had kept his wits about him enough to remember to pull out. Adding an unplanned pregnancy by a one-night stand would not be recommended.

Nick flopped next to her on the bed before he reached out to hug her to him. Cali curled against his side, throwing her right leg across his body. They laid locked in their embrace for a long time, each coming down from their high while trying to sort through their complicated emotions. It was in that quiet time, Cali's mind drifted to a thought that took hold and wouldn't let go.

"Nicholas."

"Calista."

"Why did you decide to make love to me?"

His playful chuckle helped relieve some of her fears.

"That's a rhetorical question, right? I think the real question is how could I have possibly resisted?"

"But...well... was it because of me or..." She took a deep breath before finishing her worry. "Or did you sleep with me here in Kevin's bed just to get even with him?" She was on her back in a second with Nick towering over her, his face full of anger.

"Goddammit, Cali, I'm not going to let you ruin this moment. What happened between us tonight had nothing to do with Kevin and Roni. They made their choices, and they paid for them. You're a gorgeous, intelligent woman, and I'm attracted to you. Period."

He looked serious. She wanted so badly to believe him. He eventually got up to grab a towel and a glass of water from the bathroom before pulling back the covers and getting them settled in between the cool sheets. Cali couldn't remember ever feeling more contented than she did as Nick's naked body spooned her as they both dozed off to sleep. For the first time since the accident, she fell into a dreamless sleep, free of the haunting nightmares that had been her nightly visitor since her trip to the morgue.

CHAPTER 7

*N*ick woke to the smell of coffee. It took him a few minutes to remember where he was. He reached out to find Cali's side of the bed empty but discovered the steaming cup of coffee on the bed stand. He could hear the shower running in the connected bathroom.

He'd spent the night making love to Cali in Kevin Bennett's bed. He'd awakened at two in the morning, knowing he should get up to slink home before she woke up. Instead, he had watched her sleeping peacefully in his arms, remembering how fragile she had looked as she'd begged him to stay. At the time, he had worried he was staying for all the wrong reasons. He didn't want to use Calista to get even with Kevin. She didn't deserve that.

Now, in the light of day, he knew he was in much greater danger of losing himself to her. He'd like to think this was the beginning of something special, but he feared the ugliness that had brought them together would always be wedged between them. Things were moving too fast, and he didn't know how to slow them down without hurting her.

The shower turning off moved him into motion. He got

up and scrambled to find his wrinkled clothes on the floor, rushing to throw them back on. He was sitting on the side of the bed, sipping his coffee when she emerged from the bathroom dressed in a casual yoga outfit, her wet hair wrapped in a towel. Calista was a natural beauty. Even with no makeup on, she was breathtaking.

"Good morning, sunshine." He tried to keep his voice lighter than he felt.

"Good morning, Nick. I hope I doctored your coffee the way you like it."

"It's perfect, thanks."

An awkward silence fell. Cali broke the quiet with a request.

"I was hoping you could drop me off at my car as you're leaving. I have an appointment with my real estate agent in a couple hours, then need to run a few errands."

Nick picked up on her reluctance to look him in the eye and suspected she was feeling embarrassed by her behavior the night before. He pushed to his feet and took her in his arms. She felt stiff until he stroked her back, letting his hand fall to cup her ass through the thin pants. He liked the feel of her relaxing against him. He pulled back enough so he could look into her eyes.

"How are you doing this morning? Are you feeling okay?"

She hesitated. "I'm fine, I guess. I slept better than I have since... well... you know. Thanks for staying. I'm just hoping you don't think badly of me because..."

"Shhhh." Nick cut her off with two fingers to her lips. "Don't go there. There's nothing to be embarrassed about, Cali. We're both consenting adults. I care about you."

"Oh thank goodness. I was worried I'd screwed up any chance of being able to help you with Andi. I hate being alone so much, and I really am looking forward to being able to spend time with you and your daughter. It's going to help me too."

Nick had forgotten all about that. His face must have projected his concern because Cali's face paled.

"You've changed your mind, haven't you?"

"No. I haven't. It's just... well shit. I don't want Andi to get hurt. She's already lost her mom. If I introduce her to you and she likes you, then..." He stopped, unsure how to finish the sentence without hurting Calista.

"...And then you end up regretting last night, and you'll want to avoid seeing me again."

"I'm not going to regret last night. Ever. But I do worry we're moving too fast, and we're each too emotional to be making smart decisions about new relationships. I'll never forgive myself if I end up hurting you like Kevin did."

Cali wouldn't look him in the eyes, and he suspected it was because she agreed with him. He pulled her close, cupping her face to force her to look into his eyes.

"Let's just take this one day at a time. Can we do that?"

She smiled a weak smile. "I guess so."

"Great. Now, I'm happy to take you to your car. I need to swing by and pick up Andi at her friend Katie's house, then get her to gymnastics. I know you have errands today, but would you be free to come by for dinner tonight at the house? If you're serious about babysitting with Andi, you two should meet. I'd like her to get comfortable with you before I leave town." If he'd doubted she was serious about helping him, his doubts were gone when her face lit up.

"I'd love that so much."

Cali's GPS directed her through the winding upscale subdivision lined with million-dollar homes. She was running a few minutes late for dinner with Nick and Andrea. She would have been nervous enough going to their home and meeting Nick's daughter for the first time, but spending the night before with Nick had complicated things. She was grateful he had seemed as if all was okay this morning as he'd driven her back to her car behind the Irish pub, yet she couldn't shake the fear of him having second thoughts about what they'd done as they were apart today.

She pulled into the wide driveway of the two-story brick colonial style home. It was dusk and hard to see the house number, but the front porch lights illuminated as she turned off the engine to let her know Nick was waiting for her.

Nick. Her heart did a little flip-flop as she remembered the intense look in his eyes as he'd made love to her in the middle of the night. Her memories of their passion-filled night felt surreal as if they were just a dream.

He opened the door as she walked up the sidewalk. She'd been trying to tell herself all day they'd just comforted each other the night before, but seeing him in his casual jeans and a golf shirt waiting for her with a smile had her panties getting damp in a very uncomfortable way.

"Hey, there." He leaned in for a quick kiss. "I was worried you were having trouble finding us."

"No. I just left a few minutes later than I should have. My trusty GPS got me here just fine."

Once inside, he took her jacket to the coat closet before returning to take her by the hand.

"Ready to meet Andi?"

"You bet. Does she know why I'm here?"

"Yes. We've talked about it, and she was happy you weren't like the other nannies she didn't like at all."

"But... does she know who I am?"

He stopped in his tracks, turning toward her.

"No. In fact, she doesn't know her mom was in the car

with anyone when she died. She just thinks Roni was driving."

"Okay, well I didn't plan on talking about it, anyway, but I want to be sure to back up whatever you've told her."

They went through a formal living room and an even more formal dining room before arriving at a large kitchen that opened to a comfortable family room. An oversized TV could be seen throughout the whole space. A young girl with long black hair sat in front of the TV currently playing a Disney movie.

"Andi, I've told you not to sit so close. You're gonna hurt your eyes. Come meet our guest, please."

Andrea listened to her father without complaint although she approached Cali with apprehension. As she got closer, Cali's heart contracted. She looked so much like her dad it was uncanny. It was easy to see she took after her father more than her mother which might explain why Roni hadn't bonded with her daughter as much as Nick had. Andrea's black hair and dark eyes were that of a Greek Mikos. She went to her dad, and he tucked her under his arm for a hug as he introduced them.

"Cali, I'd like you to meet my Andrea. Andi, this is a friend of mine, Cali Bennett. She's a schoolteacher and loves kids. She's agreed to help us out this week when I have to head up to New York for work. Say hello."

"Hello, Mrs. Bennett." The title kicked Cali in the gut. She hadn't been expecting it. Andi made it worse by continuing. "Are you related to the Bennett's my dad works for?"

Cali panicked, unsure how to answer. Nick came to her rescue.

"Yes, she's related to them, that's how I met her."

"Cool. Do you have any kids, Mrs. Bennett?"

"Cali. Please, just call me Cali and no, I'm afraid I don't have any kids of my own yet. Maybe one day."

73

"Do you like Elsa and Anna?"

Nick looked like he was about to apologize, but Cali cut him off.

"Of course. I love *Frozen*. I went to see it in the theater when it came out and even have a copy of my own at my house."

"You do? Really?"

"Really. I have a whole collection of Disney movies. They are some of my favorites."

"Do you have *The Little Mermaid*, too? That's my other favorite."

"Are you kidding me? That was my favorite when I was your age. No Disney collection is complete without *The Little Mermaid*."

"Wow. Can I see if you have some movies I might be missing?"

"Sure. Maybe we can watch some new movies you've never seen while your dad is out of town."

"Yippy! Can we Dad? Can I stay up watching movies on a school night?"

Cali grinned as she turned to Nick. "Yeah, Nick. Can we stay up watching movies on a school night?"

Nick chuckled. "Wow, you've been here three minutes, and I'm already getting ganged up on by you two. The normal rules apply. You get your homework done in time, then sure. You can watch movies until bedtime. Now, I think we'd better eat dinner before the lasagna burns. Andi, set the table please."

"Okay, Dad."

She skipped off to the kitchen leaving Cali and Nick. He whispered to her, "That went well."

"How could it not? She's perfect, Nick. You must be so proud."

"Wait until you see her in the morning trying to get her

out the door to catch the school bus, and we'll see what you say then. That's the one thing she got from Roni. They are both the antithesis of morning people."

"Well, if I don't have my coffee, I'm the same so watch out."

"I don't know." He kept his voice down to make sure Andi couldn't hear him. "You didn't scare me this morning."

"I was on my best behavior."

Dinner was a fun affair with Nick quizzing Andi and Cali on their Disney trivia. Cali was impressed with how bright and happy Andrea was, considering she had just lost her mom a few months before. It was a blessing she was taking her loss in stride.

Andi's inquiry brought her back to the conversation at hand.

"Do you have *Hercules* in your collection, Cali?"

"Of course. It was always one of my favorites too since my parents are from Greece."

"Wow! My family is from Greece, too. Dad says we're going to go there on vacation one day. Since your family is from there too, maybe you can come with us!"

Cali's stomach churned with a sudden flood of memories that inevitably snuck up on her when she least expected it.

Nick noticed. "Hey, you okay?"

Calista forced a calming breath. Andi couldn't have known that she had accidentally opened a hornet's nest of unpleasant memories.

"I'm fine. I was just... I've been to Greece many times. We used to go when I was a kid to visit my grandparents." Andi had no clue Calista wanted to change the subject.

"That's so exciting. I checked out a library book about Greece. Dad said I needed to study up on it before I go there so I can be his tour guide. Maybe you can be our tour guide."

"I don't think that's a good idea," Cali stammered. "I'm

sure you'll make a wonderful tour guide."

Andrea let the subject drop and launched herself into her dad's lap for tickles. While father and daughter bonded, Cali fought back tears. She wanted to cry that she was alone—she didn't have Kevin's child to help her stave off her loneliness now that he was gone. She wanted to cry at the drudged up painful memories of her last visit to her grandparents and how that trip had changed her life forever. She wanted to cry because, for the first time since she arrived, she felt like an outsider—like she was intruding on their private family moment.

Nick sensed she was turning melancholy and lifted Andi to her own feet.

"Okay, let's clear the table, then you can finish watching your show before you need to go up and take a shower."

"But Dad, it's Saturday night. It's early!"

"I didn't say you had to go to bed yet."

"Can we play Wii?"

Nick glanced at Cali. "You mind?"

"Not at all. In fact, I'd love to learn."`

The next two hours flew by. Andi dragged Cali up to give her the grand tour of her bedroom and bathroom. After her shower, Cali helped Andi comb out her long, tangled hair, giving her tips on how to keep the tangles down since she had similar hair. They ended the night playing several games on the Wii. Cali may have lost every game, but she couldn't remember having as much fun as she had tonight. She was almost as disappointed as Andi when Nick announced it was Andrea's bedtime.

"But Dad, can't I stay up later tonight? I want to teach Cali how to golf on the Wii."

"I'm sure Cali can wait until next week to learn how to golf on the Wii. You need to get to bed so we can get you up and out to Sunday School in the morning."

Cali was unprepared for Andrea to throw herself into her lap. The goodnight hug the young girl gave her warmed her heart more than she thought possible. Her eyes locked with Nick's behind Andi's back. The smile that lit up his face was anything but parental, reminding her they would be alone again once his daughter was asleep.

Nick was gone for fifteen minutes putting Andi to bed. Cali used the time to try to sort through her complicated emotions. Spending time with Nick and his daughter had made her own loneliness worse. She knew it was petty and she hated herself when she felt real jealousy Nick had Andi to help ease the pain from the loss of his wife.

"She's finally down. She was talking a mile a minute about all the things she wants to do with you when I'm out of town. I sure hope you haven't changed your mind." Nick had gone to the kitchen island and was opening a new bottle of wine.

"Of course I haven't changed my mind," Cali called over to him from the living room couch. "She's adorable. It'll be nice to have something new to do this week to break the monotony."

An awkward silence descended while Nick poured two glasses of wine before heading over to sit near Calista. He handed her a glass before sitting a few feet away, angling his body toward her so he could watch her as they spoke. She felt self-conscious as they sat silently sipping their wine. They hadn't talked about the night before yet. Not really. She struggled to start the conversation.

"She's really great, Nick. You're so lucky to have her." Okay, so maybe those weren't the right words because she found herself tearing up with unnamed emotion.

"I know. It's a miracle."

"Why do you say that?"

It was Nick's turn to look uncomfortable. He chugged

down half of his wine before he continued.

"Remember, I wasn't married to Roni when she got pregnant. In fact, we had broken up for several months. I only found out about Andrea when Veronica showed up on my doorstep with a baby in tow. To say I was surprised is an understatement."

"But you decided to marry her, anyway?"

"Yeah. It seemed like the right thing to do for everyone involved. I figured we'd settle down. Maybe have a few more kids. Live the dream, you know?"

Cali wasn't sure how to respond. "Some dream. Andi is eight now, right? You decided not to have any more kids after all?"

"I didn't decide that, but Roni apparently did. I thought we were trying. She even had me convinced it was my fault it wasn't working."

"If you read my texts, you know we were trying and couldn't get pregnant either. Seems our spouses had that in common, too."

"I am sorry, Cali. I do feel bad I read those texts from Kevin." He finished off his wine before continuing. "If it makes you feel better, I think Roni got the last laugh on this one. Last week her OBGYN office called to find out why she had missed her regularly scheduled Depo-Provera shot."

"But... isn't that?"

"Yep. The bitch actually made me feel guilty I couldn't get her pregnant again. I hung up the phone that day a changed man. That's the day I knew my mourning for her was over. It was the day I knew Andi and I were gonna be better off without her." The vehemence as he spoke the bitter words shocked Cali. He had been looking away but turned his eyes to bore into her as he continued with passion. "You may not believe it yet, Cali, but you're gonna be better off without Kevin too. He was a prick. He didn't deserve you."

Her breath caught in her chest as she whispered, "Is that why you came to see me yesterday?"

His dark eyes were devouring her as he reached out to hold her hand resting on the couch between them.

"It was part of it, yes. I mean, yes, I do need your help this week but..." Nick set his empty wine glass on the coffee table before shifting closer to Cali. She was unprepared for him to reach up and cup her face gently, holding her face in a way that made it impossible for her to look away. "But mainly, it was because I find myself thinking of you at the strangest times. While I'm in meetings or at the gym. I ran through a stop sign the other day because I was daydreaming about you. I must have picked up the phone ten times to call you before I finally did."

"Me? Why? You don't owe me anything, Nick."

"Dammit, Cali, this isn't about owing you."

"What is it about then?"

"Damned if I know. All I know is I feel close to you. Even before last night."

"Nick, that's natural. We've both gone through the same hell. We're the only ones who really understand what the other is going through."

"It's more than that, baby. Didn't you feel it tonight?"

"I felt a lot of things tonight." Cali's heart contracted with his endearment. "I'm more confused than ever."

Cali went without protest as Nick pulled her into his arms to sit on his lap. She felt the steady rhythm of his beating heart as she snuggled against his chest. She was relieved he didn't push for more answers. They sat silently, holding each other, each lost in thought, Nick's gentle caresses on her lower back relaxing her. For the first time in a very long time, Cali felt at peace.

It wasn't until she detected Nick's erection growing under her bottom that her thoughts returned to their passionate night before. Nick's seduction was subtle as he nuzzled her hair, sucking her earlobe into his mouth before he trailed sweet kisses down her neck. Her heart rate spiked as she recognized her core clenching with need.

When she lifted her face, Nick captured her lips in a hard kiss as his other hand grasped a nipple through her clothes, pinching hard enough to draw a whimper from deep within. The room felt too warm as their body temperatures rose with building sexual tension.

Relief coursed through Cali as she felt Nick's hands exploring her body, igniting the same passionate feelings they had felt the night before. She'd worried he would think ill of her for her aggressive pursuit of him twenty-four hours earlier. Tonight, he was the aggressor as his hand groped between her legs, stroking her labia through her jeans.

He stood with her still cradled in his arms. Throwing her arms around his collar, she burrowed into his neck as he carried her silently through the darkened house. He passed the stairs to the second floor, electing to go down a hall instead.

Nick struggled to open a six-panel wood door. Once inside the dimly lit room, she recognized they were in his home office. He stopped to lock the door before carrying her to the large wooden desk with neatly piled stacks of files. They didn't speak as he set Cali down on the edge of the desk before reaching to swipe the paperwork aside, causing several piles to flutter to the floor.

He was moving faster as if his control was slipping. Their brown eyes locked as Nick grabbed the hem of her blouse, pulling it over her head and tossing it aside. He lunged forward to cup her breasts through her bra, stooping to kiss the rounded curves protruding above the lacy trim. When he yanked the fabric below the swell of her globes, he bared her nipples, and they were pushed up at attention. Cali held him to her tightly, enjoying the feel of his tongue sucking her greedily.

When Cali reached to pull his tucked shirt out of the waist of his jeans, he released her nip long enough to allow the shirt to be pulled over his head. His lips were back on her hardened tips as he unhooked her bra and threw it to the floor.

She spread her legs wide, so he could nuzzle close. He yanked her ass to the edge of the desk before pressing her body to lay back. The desk was just wide enough for her torso and head to fit. Nick's hands moved to her zipper, divesting Cali of her jeans and panties within seconds, leaving her sprawled naked across the top.

Cali lifted her heels to the edge to the desk, bending her knees, the position leaving her splayed open for her lover to claim her sex with his mouth. When she reached down to fist his hair, Nick glanced up into her eyes with a devastatingly sexy grin. The desire she saw mirrored back at her had her pussy clenching to be filled.

"Stretch your arms out, hold on to the edges of the desk, and don't let go." Nick's voice was gruff as he took charge of the scene.

Cali did as he asked, feeling the familiar tug of submission. She had learned firsthand how thin the line was between dominance and abuse in a relationship. Her husband had crossed the line more times than she could count. As odd as it was, she trusted Nick in a way she had never trusted Kevin. She opened herself, yielding every intimate part over to the man who was eating her out with gusto.

He pulled her lower lips apart, baring her wet core for his inspection just before he nudged her clit with the tip of his tongue. She bucked her ass off the desk to thrust up against his warm mouth. He answered by plunging two fingers deep into her tight channel, curling them just enough to find her g-spot, tipping her into her first orgasm of the night within seconds.

Cali was still in a haze when she felt his tongue move lower to rim the tight ring of her anus. She had never been on the receiving end of this intimate act. She wanted to feel embarrassed, but it felt too damn good. He slid his hands lower to spread her ass cheeks wide, allowing his tongue to venture into her tightest hole. The sexual act was raw... intimate... naughty. It made it that much more exciting.

She had closed her eyes to enjoy the new sensations, so she was unprepared for a thick digit, coated with her own juices, sliding effortlessly into her tightest hole. Cali squealed with delight as the pleasurable fullness surprised her. Kevin had used her ass for his rough sport many times. He had even been able to wring orgasms out of her by applying pressure to her clit as he sodomized his wife. Never had he made her feel like she felt at this moment—she almost panicked. Nick chose that moment to peer up at her, his mouth still on her pussy, his fingers shoved in her tight hole—his eyes pierced her heart. The raw heat she saw there melted her to a pool of sexual need. She heard herself pleading for more.

"Nick, please..."

He answered by adding a second finger to her ass. It still didn't hurt, but she was acutely aware of her body stretching to accommodate the new intrusion. Her lover's domination of her body continued until Cali shattered into pieces across the desk. As she lay boneless in her recovery, she sensed Nick moving away from her and heard the rustling of his remaining clothes falling to the floor. The room fell silent, so when she felt him behind the desk near her head, she opened her eyes to look up at a hard erection jutting inches above her with Nick's grinning face just beyond.

He spoke for the first time in several long minutes. "I'm

going to fuck your mouth now, baby." It wasn't a question, it was a command, and it shocked her and thrilled her in equal measure. She remained still, allowing him to manhandle her body closer to the other side of the desk, pulling her toward him until her head was no longer supported by the hard-wood. He helped her head fall back, presenting her mouth for his consumption.

The idea of him using her mouth to pleasure himself excited Cali. As he moved his body closer, she got her first close-up view of his heavy sac hanging below his thick rod. Nick had to bend his knees to put the tip of his erection against her lips. She opened reflexively, welcoming his cock as he slowly slid inside her, and his hands reached forward to squeeze her breasts.

He allowed her several shallow insertions to get used to his thickness. Each stroke went a bit deeper until she finally felt him nudging the back of her throat. Her body revolted with a gag that had phlegm flooding her mouth and coating Nick's cock.

He set a steady pace that kept the back of her head pinned against the hardness of the desk. She surrendered to his facial fucking, trusting him implicitly to pull out to allow her deep breaths of precious air. Each break for air had new strings of phlegm spilling from her mouth. She wanted to be embarrassed at the mess they were making, but the pleasur-able groans he was emitting told her he was enjoying their session just as it was.

Cali was prepared to drink his cum, but Nick had other ideas. Her throat felt raw from his rough use by the time he stepped away from her to move to the other side of the desk again. He pulled her body back, so her head was resting on the desk before grabbing a condom packet on the desk she had failed to notice before now. The protection slid on easily. He pulled her ass off the desk, pushing her bent legs far apart and back toward her chest, opening her core to him completely.

Their eyes met before he claimed her. There was so much emotion there, she couldn't interpret it.

"Are you doing okay, baby?" His question surprised her. "Still with me?"

"Better than okay. Take me... please. I need you inside me, Nick." Her voice rasped from his use of her throat.

Her words pleased him, and his eyes consumed her as he warned, "Don't let go, Cali."

It was hard to hold her position when Nick's carnality had him surging forward in one swift stroke. She fought to keep her wide hold on to the edges of the desk as he plummeted her tightness. She was so wet, their coupling made slurping noises in the otherwise quiet room. Only Nick's occasional grunts of exertion from his fast fucking joined the soundtrack.

"Come with me, Cali. I want to watch you fly, baby."

Always a good girl, she did as he demanded. She arched her back as they both cried out their climax. Several minutes went by as Nick slumped over Cali's body, still connected in the most intimate of ways. He captured her lips in a tender kiss just as she felt his softening cock slip from her body. She finally released the edges of the desk to hug him tightly.

Nick broke the silence with a quiet, "Wow."

Cali couldn't help but giggle. "Double wow."

As intense as their lovemaking had been, Nick pulled her up before lifting her into his arms to carry her the few feet to the comfortable chair near the door. They snuggled quietly, each lost in thought. Cali's last thought before she drifted off to sleep was how grateful she was to Kevin for cheating on her with Veronica, or she would have never met the amazing man holding her tightly in his arms.

CHAPTER 8

"Come on, girls! We need to get moving, or I'm gonna miss my flight!"

Nick wasn't finished with his sentence before Cali and Andi appeared at the top of the winding staircase. His heart lurched at the sight of the two most important people in his life. Not for the first time, he marveled at how quickly his life had changed.

He was aware that to many, he was disrespecting his dead wife by moving on with his life so quickly, but considering the circumstances of her death and how she had chosen to betray him at every turn, he felt zero guilt. In fact, he had ceased being angry with his wife and her lover at all. By his estimation, they had done him and Cali a favor—were it not for their sordid affair, he never would have gotten to know the amazing woman walking down the stairs, deep in conversation with his daughter.

When they reached the bottom step, Andi held out a sheet of paper.

"Don't forget to sign this Dad. We're going on that field trip into the city today, and you forgot to sign the paper when you gave me the money to go. Mrs. Fields said I have to stay behind with the first graders if you don't sign."

"Oh no!" Nick grabbed a pen from his briefcase and quickly scribbled his signature. "We can't let you spend the day with those first graders." He addressed Cali as he handed the paper to his daughter. "I hope you don't mind, but I added you to Andi's emergency contact list at the school. That way you can sign permission slips like this if you need to when I'm out of town."

Pleasure lit up her brown eyes, the golden flecks visible in the sunlight filtering in the front windows.

"Thanks, but what if I sign something you disagree with?"

"You won't, and since we text ten times a day, anyway, just ask if you're not sure."

Cali picked up her own briefcase and purse from the front table. Nick reached to hand her a travel mug of coffee, and they all headed to the garage. They'd already developed a comfortable routine in the three weeks since Cali had been acting as their nanny. A surge of guilt hit him as he remembered canceling an interview with another nanny from the service the day before. He knew he was taking advantage of Calista's willingness to help him out, but he suspected she didn't mind.

In fact, she'd practically moved into the guest bedroom. The first week she had just stayed at the house with Andi the few days he was out of town, but each subsequent week, she'd stayed more frequently. He couldn't resist sleeping in the guest room with her most nights, setting his alarm for extra early to get up and slink back to his own room before Andi awoke. They both knew they were playing with fire, but as each week passed, he worried less about Andi finding out they were dating since his daughter adored Calista as much as he did.

Nick drove the family van as they dropped Andi at her

school first, then drove to the airport. They had just enough time to drop him off for his flight and get Cali back to her school.

When they got to the airport, Cali jumped out to jog to the driver's side. They embraced for a long goodbye kiss before the police officer directing traffic whistled at them to move along.

Nick gazed into her eyes as he said his goodbyes. "I'll be home tomorrow night."

"Okay, text me the details. Andi and I will pick you up together, and maybe we could stop to grab a bite on the way home."

Nick didn't miss her use of the word 'home.' She hadn't officially moved in, but he'd noticed the house didn't feel the same when she wasn't there. They needed to talk about where things were headed soon, but as the car horns around them reminded him, now was not the time nor place.

"That sounds like a plan. I'll call you later." With a last kiss, he grabbed his carry-on bag and headed into the terminal.

Nick was led into the boardroom where a half-dozen men and women in suits were waiting for him. He dropped his briefcase on the table before turning to the redheaded assistant ushering him to the meeting.

"Thanks, Jane. You wouldn't have a place I could plug my phone in, would you?"

Nick's flight to New York had been delayed, and he was late arriving at his client's office. He'd drained the battery replying to emails in the terminal.

"Sure thing, Mr. Mikos. Let me plug it in out at my desk."

Nick handed his dead phone to the attractive administrative assistant and turned his attention to the meeting about to begin.

Not fifteen minutes later, a pale Jane stepped back into the meeting. She tried not to interrupt, but since Nick was leading the discussion, it was impossible.

A feeling of dread washed over him when his eyes connected with Jane's when he saw panic and pity shining back at him. He stopped talking mid-sentence, waiting for her to lean down and whisper into his ear.

"I'm so sorry... your phone is charging... I think you need to step out and make a call."

"Can it wait? As you can see, I'm a critical participant this morning."

"No sir, it can't wait." Her voice broke as if she were holding back tears. "You need to call Calista right away."

His heart lurched at the unexpected sound of Cali's name in this setting. It only took a few seconds to know something was really wrong. Cali should be in class teaching. There was no way she'd call unless there was an emergency. Memories of receiving other bad news when the police had shown up on his doorstep a few months before came next, but they were quickly overshadowed by the realization the only thing Cali could be calling about was Andi.

Nick stumbled to his feet, barely getting out a short, "Excuse me" as he followed Jane out of the boardroom. Each step he took felt like it was his last.

He unlocked his phone to find several missed calls, voice-mail messages, and text messages. They had started while he was in the air on his flight. He'd expected to see Cali's number there, but the fact the first messages had come from Andi's school had him collapsing into the chair near Jane's desk.

He tried to rationalize there could be many reasons for

them to call. Perhaps Andi had a headache or stomach ache. But he'd hugged her, and she hadn't felt like she had a temperature this morning.

The first message was vague.

"Mr. Mikos, this is Andrea's school calling. Please call into the office as soon as possible."

The second message from the school was more ominous.

"Mr. Mikos, this is Mrs. Peterson calling from Andi's school. We really need you to contact us as soon as possible."

Fuck. The principal herself called.

Cali's messages were worse.

"Nick, I need you to call me right away. I just got a call from Andi' school. Nick... there's been an accident on the field trip. I don't have any details yet, but I'm heading to the hospital now to be there with her. Call me as soon as you get this... please."

An accident. Another fucking accident. The first one robbed him of his wife. Not Andrea. Not his Andi.

He said a short prayer that Andi was fine before he pressed play on Cali's next message.

"Nick. Oh God, I need to talk to you. I don't want to leave this in a message. I'm at the hospital, and they won't tell me anything about Andi, but there are lots of other parents coming in here too. I'm trying to find out more. Call me. Please."

The fear in her voice told him how serious things were. He felt numb. He knew he should call her right away, but he took a long minute, praying it wasn't the last minute where he knew his daughter was still with him on this earth. Losing Roni had hurt, but losing Andrea would kill him. He was sure of it.

He felt the tears silently trekking down his cheeks as he pressed Cali's number in his contact list. He reached to accept the tissue Jane was holding out to him as he heard Cali's panicked voice answer the call.

"Oh thank God you called. I've been frantic I couldn't reach you."

The lump in his throat kept him from responding.

"Nick?"

He finally forced the words out. "God, Cali. Please tell me she's okay. Tell me the truth. Is my baby okay?"

"I had trouble at first getting updates from the hospital, but the administrator from the school showed up and confirmed I was on Andi's emergency contact list, so the nurse has started giving me updates. Andi's alive Nick, but she was unconscious when they brought her in and... well... they had to take her into surgery."

"Surgery? What for? Where are her injuries?"

"It's chaos here with a busload of kids and their families, so I'm afraid I don't know too many details about why they're doing surgery. They promised me they'd send someone out with an update as soon as they can, but she went in over thirty minutes ago."

His heart was pounding. He forced himself to focus. Covering the phone, he asked Jane to go into the boardroom and collect up all of his belongings and bring them out after letting the group know he had to leave for a family emergency. He then returned his attention to Cali. He could hear her crying at the other end of the phone and knew she needed him to be strong for her. He was so grateful she was there for his and Andi's sake.

"I'm on my way back. I'll get the first flight I can and be there as soon as possible. Text me the details of the hospital, and I'll take a cab there when I land. Cali?"

"Yes." Her answer was a whisper.

"I'm so glad you're there, honey. I'm sorry you have to go through this again so soon after..."

"Don't you dare compare this to Kevin and Roni's accident." Her angry reply surprised Nick. "They got what they deserved. Andi is an innocent. A perfect, beautiful baby who deserves to have a full life ahead of her."

"And she will, Cali. We have to think positive. She's in the right place, and the doctors are going to take care of her. I need you to stay calm for Andrea's sake. Call me with updates. I'm on my way, baby."

He heard her sob at the other end. "Nick. Please. Be careful. I can't take any more people I love getting hurt."

It seemed like an odd time to tell him she loved him. He knew for a fact he'd fallen in love with her and had held off telling her, only so he didn't rush her. That suddenly felt like a dumb reason.

"I love you, Calista. I promise. I'll be there soon, baby." He pressed end before rushing out the door to head back to the airport. He needed to get home to his girls.

CHAPTER 9

*C*ali reached to accept the cup of bitter coffee from the school administrator who was trying to make herself useful to the parents crowded into the hospital waiting room. In fairness, the representatives from the school were as upset as the other loved ones waiting for updates on their children.

The group had just finished listening to an informal update from the local police chief with more details of what had happened. There were still a lot of unanswered questions, but it appeared the driver of a semi-truck had lost control of his rig and rear-ended the stopped school bus, pushing the bus through a downed crossing guard and into the path of a speeding commuter train. The bus driver had been pronounced dead on the scene, and the most seriously injured children had been seated in the front of the bus where the impact occurred, but since the bus had flipped to its side, all the children had been injured in some way. Cali held onto the hope Andi had been sitting closer to the back. They hadn't announced any children had died... yet.

She sat with her eyes glued to the door of the waiting

room, not sure if she was praying for Nick to arrive first or a doctor with an update from the surgery. Andi had been in the operating room for over three hours with no word on her condition. Cali told herself no news was good news, yet she'd noticed several of the families had already collected their banged-up children and were starting to leave. With each departure, the group waiting got more solemn as they were the families of the more seriously injured.

When Cali finally spotted Nicholas rushing down the long hallway toward the glass door to the waiting room, she almost fainted with relief. She'd only known Andrea for a short time, but she already loved Nick's daughter. She couldn't even imagine the fear Nick must be feeling with his only child in danger.

Cali ran to the door to meet him. They fell into each other's arms, hugging each other so tightly, they were both short of breath, the sobs she had been valiantly holding back bubbling over.

"I am so sorry, Nick. I didn't do a very good job taking care of Andi for you."

He pulled back so he could see her eyes. She saw terror there.

"Why are you sorry? Do you have news I don't know? Is she....?"

"No! I'm sorry. I didn't mean to make it sound like that. I'm still waiting for the doctor to come find me after surgery. It's just that..."

He cut her off. "Stop. This isn't your fault, Cali. This would have happened if I'd been in town, too. Not another word about you not taking care of Andi. You got the school's call and made sure to reach me. You've been here, waiting."

"A lot of good it did. They only let me see her briefly, and she wasn't even conscious."

They'd barely moved into the room when a young doctor

in blue scrubs came in and asked, "Is the family of Andrea Mikos here?"

They were holding hands, and he pulled her back toward the door with him as he answered. "Yes, I'm her father. How is my baby girl?"

The doctor glanced around the room full of other families and elected to move them to another location. "Let's step across the hall into the consultation room. We'll have more privacy there."

Nick squeezed Cali's hand so hard, it was cutting off the circulation, but she didn't mind. She knew he was thinking the same thing. Why would they need to relocate if the news was good? The tension in the tiny room was thick. The doctor looked nervous, another bad sign.

"I'm Doctor Adams, and I operated on Andrea today. It was a long surgery as we had to do some exploration once we were in the OR. I'm not going to lie. Andrea is going to have a few rough days ahead of her, but I have every expectation she's going to come through okay."

"Oh thank God." Nick pulled Cali into his arms for a hug they both needed. Relief coursed through Cali at the news Andrea was alive and expected to recover.

The doctor gave them a minute before he continued with his report.

"As I understand it, Andrea was sitting near the front of the bus where some of the more seriously injured students were located. She was unconscious when she was brought in, and her vital signs were plummeting quickly which usually indicates internal bleeding. We didn't have time to do a CT scan or other tests, so I took her into surgery immediately to find the root cause of her bleeding."

The doctor took a short break to look at his buzzing cell phone before continuing with his update. "I'm afraid I had to remove her spleen. It was badly damaged in the collision. She also has several cracked ribs, but they should heal quickly in a child her age, and her ribs didn't puncture her lungs which is always a concern with impact collisions. Andrea also had a small laceration to her liver I repaired."

"Oh my God, that sounds so serious. What's the prognosis with her losing her spleen?" Nick pressed for answers.

"We're starting her on antibiotics right away, and she'll most likely need to stay on them for some time. A person without a spleen will always be more prone to infection than average, but she should recover fully from all of those injuries. She did lose enough blood we had to give her blood transfusions during the surgery and will most likely do one more in a couple of hours. With all the trauma's coming in, I'm afraid we were a bit short on Andrea's blood type."

"I'd like to donate my blood for her if possible."

"Of course. That would be good since we're running short although we won't be able to use your blood until it goes through the normal processing. Still, it'll be good to get some on standby in case she needs more in a few days. I'll have a nurse come and cross-check your blood types after we're finished talking."

"If you're running short on blood," Cali broke in, "I'm happy to donate too."

"Great. I'll have you both setup then. I'm afraid I haven't finished my update though."

Nick and Cali looked at each other nervously before letting the doctor continue his report.

"As I said, Andrea was unconscious when they brought her in. She has a large contusion on her left temple and a pretty deep cut on her left shoulder. She has significant swelling of her brain, and I'm electing to keep her sedated for at least the next twenty-four hours to give her body time to heal and the swelling to come down. The CT scan doesn't show any major brain damage, so I have every reason to believe she'll be cognitively healthy once she recovers, but as with most head injuries, we won't know for sure until she regains consciousness, and we can do more tests."

"Wait, so she's going to be unconscious for at least the next twenty-four hours?" Cali blurted the question, then looked at Nick to see if he was angry she was injecting on behalf of his daughter. She shouldn't have worried. He looked relieved she'd asked.

"Yes, keeping her sedated will give her brain time to recover from the trauma. With a concussion this severe, she'll need several weeks to truly recover."

"When can we see her, doctor?" Nick was squeezing her hand tightly again.

"She's still in post-op. She'll be there for another hour or two, then we'll move her to the pediatric ICU. You'll be able to see your daughter once they get her settled there." The doctor stood, making ready to leave. He turned from the door to address them.

"I know parents don't expect to have their children injured like this when they send them off to school in the morning, but all things considered, Andrea was lucky today. From what I've seen of some of the other children they brought in, it could have been even worse. I'll come check in with you up in the ICU later, Mr. and Mrs. Mikos."

He opened the door and was gone before they could correct him on his assumption that Cali was Nick's wife. Nick sat so still, she worried he'd gone into shock. She tried to cup his face, but he was in a trance. Cali moved to his lap, snuggling tight against him as they sat in silence, comforting each other for several long minutes until a nurse stuck her head in.

"Mr. and Mrs. Mikos? Dr. Adams asked me to take you down to have your blood drawn. If you'd follow me, please, I'll take you to the lab."

They followed the nurse, and once in the elevator, Cali quietly corrected the nurse. "I'm not Mrs. Mikos. I'm not Andi's mom, but I'd still like to donate blood for anyone else who might need it."

"I'm sorry." The nurse looked embarrassed for her false assumption. "Is Andrea's mother on her way here then?"

Nick answered, his voice harsh. "Her mother is dead."

"I'm so sorry."

Nick pulled Cali close before answering, "Don't be sorry."

They were led to a small room with several tall stools often seen in blood labs. A phlebotomist greeted them, and they spent several minutes filling out paperwork. It took only twenty minutes for them both to finish and be led back up to the waiting room closest to the pediatric ICU. There were several other parents already waiting there, and Nick was upset to find the parents of Andi's best friend, Katie there. The girls had been seated on the bus together so it made sense they'd both suffered similar injuries. Like Andi, Katie was expected to recover, but in addition to a concussion, she had a broken arm and several deep cuts.

It was two hours later when a nurse came to collect Nick for his first visit with his daughter. Cali wasn't sure if they would let her in, but Nick wouldn't hear of leaving her behind.

Andi looked so fragile. She was pale, and they had her under a heating blanket to keep her warm. She had a large bandage on her head as well as her left shoulder. They couldn't see the bandages from the surgery, but that was probably for the best. The sound of the monitoring system she was attached to was strangely comforting to Cali, knowing it would alert the nurses to any emergency. Nick had pulled the sole chair next to the bed to take her tiny hand in his own when the blood pressure cuff on her right arm filled to take her blood pressure.

"Daddy's here, baby." Tears streamed down Nick's face as he talked to his daughter. "Everything's going to be okay. You just need to sleep for a while to let your body heal. The doctor says you're gonna be as good as new. Cali is here with me. We're gonna be right here when you wake up. I'm not going to leave until I can take you home with me."

She could tell he was trying his best to keep his voice strong for Andi's sake. Neither of them knew if she could hear them, but they talked to her, nonetheless.

Minutes stretched to hours as they ran out of things to talk to Andi about. The drone of the machines monitoring the patient was the only sound as they kept their watch on the little girl they both loved.

Cali observed Nick closely. She knew he was on the edge. Eventually, they both needed to eat something and take a break. It took her several attempts to convince him he needed to step away long enough to at least grab some coffee. Cali knew it took all of Nick's strength to leave Andi behind in that bed without him there.

They were walking hand-in-hand by the nursing station in the middle of the unit when Andi's doctor looked up from the chart he was writing in and stopped them. He looked uncomfortable as if he had bad news.

"Mr. Mikos, if you have a minute, I'd like to speak with you about your daughter."

"Of course. Do you have any news about how long you'll be leaving her sedated? I'm anxious to have her wake up."

"That's understandable, but it's best for her to get past the worst of the pain while sedated. She's going to be in significant discomfort when she wakes up."

"Damn, I hadn't really thought of that. You're right."

Dr. Adams led them to an isolated alcove and paused before he asked a question that confused Cali. "I wanted to ask you how old Andrea was when you adopted her?"

"Andi wasn't adopted. What makes you think that she was?"

The doctor looked back and forth between them, looking more uncomfortable by the minute. He finally continued. "We, of course, have to do blood type cross matching before every transfusion. Your daughter is a type O- which is actually a pretty common blood type."

"That's good."

"Yes, except she's only able to accept blood from other type-O donors."

"Okay. So is that a problem? I'm not sure what type I am."

"You're a type AB, Mr. Mikos. That's a very rare type, and I'm afraid we won't be able to use your blood for your daughter. It'll be added to the blood bank."

Nick looked disappointed. "That's fine. She must have gotten her blood type from her mother then."

"Perhaps, it's just... well I'm not sure how to tell you this. I know you've already received a lot of bad news today, but I feel it important to tell you that based on the blood work, there's no possible way you could be Andrea's biological father."

CHAPTER 10

*N*ick felt his legs giving way beneath him. He would have collapsed if Cali hadn't propped him up. His mind reeled as Calista and the doctor helped him navigate back to the waiting room which was thankfully empty. Only after he sank to a chair did the doctor apologize.

"I'm so sorry. Maybe I shouldn't have told you. I just thought you had the right to know. I encourage you to have additional testing done to reconfirm the results."

Nick was in shock. He wanted to scream at the doctor that he was wrong. To even contemplate he was right was unfathomable. He was Andi's father. She looked so much like him.

The doctor was moving to leave when Nick snapped out of it enough to remember to ask, "Do you at least have O type blood for Andi's transfusion?"

He turned back toward them. "Yes, as I said, type O is pretty common. In fact, Ms. Bennett is a type O. We saved her blood to have on reserve for your daughter."

Nick felt a small measure of relief. He wasn't sure how

long he sat lost in a sea of memories. His mind raced to recall every detail leading up to Veronica showing up with Andrea in her arms to tell him he was a father. What a fool he'd been to believe her story, yet even now, he was thankful for her lie —he couldn't imagine his life without Andrea in it.

A fierce urge to find the truth consumed him. Only when he found the truth would he be able to take action to ensure Andrea would remain safely at his side the rest of his life. With Roni dead, there was no way to wrestle the truth out of her. He'd have to get help.

"Nick. I'm worried about you. Please, talk to me."

Cali's soft pleas finally broke through his dark thoughts. He looked up to see worry etched on her face. He saw relief in her eyes when he acknowledged her. He suspected she'd been talking to him before, but he'd been too consumed with his worry to hear her.

"I have no words." That was the most truthful reply he could come up with.

"Maybe it's a mistake. I think you should have an actual paternity test done to be sure."

He didn't answer right away. His mind was reeling as a wave of hatred consumed him.

"I'm glad she's dead. She deserved to die."

"You don't mean that."

"Yes, I do. From the very beginning, she played me. Everything we had for the last eight years was a lie."

"Maybe, but she also gave you Andi. I've seen you with her, and I don't care what any test tells us, you're Andrea's father. The only one she's going to have. If it took Veronica to lie to you to have Andi in your life, it was worth it. Right?"

He couldn't deny her logic. The thought of losing Andi had the lump in his throat almost choking him. Cali seemed to notice and silently moved to sit in his lap. He squeezed her to him as if she were his lifeline, and when she snuggled into his neck, her tenderness broke the delicate thread he'd been holding onto his sanity with.

Nick let the sobs he'd been holding back wrack his body as he cried for his daughter's injuries... for the loss of his marriage... the loss of his innocent trust of a woman who had built their life on lies... But mostly, he cried out of fear of losing the baby girl he would give his life for.

Nick had never allowed himself to lose control like this in his entire life. As he slowly gained command of his emotions, he became embarrassed for his show of weakness in front of Calista. She'd been through hell herself. She needed him to be strong.

As he collected himself, he apologized. "I'm so sorry I lost it."

Calista reached up to cup his face, pulling him to face her. He saw her own tears glistening, but what surprised him the most was her love shining back at him.

"Of course you did. Your world is unraveling."

"I love you, Cali. I'm so glad you're here with me. I can't even think about going through this without you here."

"Oh, Nick, I love you too. I just wish there was more I could do."

"You're doing it. Just be here with me. Please."

"I'm not going anywhere."

Nick and Cali passed the time as best as they could while keeping watch over the unconscious Andi. They took turns talking to her, telling her stories of the fun things they would be doing together when she got out of the hospital.

By eleven that night, Nick forced Cali to go home and get

some rest. She wouldn't hear of leaving until he asked her to stop by his house to pick up some things for him on the way back to the hospital the next day. He knew giving her something to do, it would help her feel less guilty about taking off for a while.

Nick needed for her to leave so he could put the plan he'd been hatching into motion. As soon as she left, he pulled out his phone to look through his contact list. He was relieved to find the name he was looking for. He pushed send and waited for an answer.

"This is Blackburn."

"Jason, this is Nicholas Mikos. I'm sorry to disturb you at this hour, but I need your help."

"Nick, you ought to know I work crazy hours in my job. This is actually a good time. I'm just sitting parked and could use a good distraction. Your firm need some help again?"

"No. I have a personal problem I need some help with this time."

"Shit. I'm sorry to hear that. When people call me with personal problems, that's never a good thing."

"You're right. It isn't good. It's critical that you're discreet. I honestly don't know how big of a hornet's nest I'm gonna find, but it's crucial I'm the only one who's aware of your findings."

"You don't need to lecture me, counselor. Discretion is my middle name. I wouldn't be in business if it wasn't." Nick heard the defensive tone in the private detective's voice and knew he'd insulted him with his warning.

"Understood and thanks. So how does this work?"

"Why don't you start from the beginning? What's the problem we're trying to solve? Is it your wife? Stepping out on you?"

Nick's unwanted manic laughter reminded him how close to the surface his emotions still were.

"I don't need your help to prove that. My wife died in a car accident over three months ago. She was riding in a car after midnight with her lover and proceeded to bite his cock off during the impact of their accident. No, she did a fine job of hanging herself on that one."

"Ouch. That's cold. I'm sorry, man. So if not infidelity, how can I help?"

"My eight-year-old daughter was in an accident today. She's going to be okay, but she's in the hospital. During testing, her paternity has come into question. The hospital is claiming I couldn't be her biological father based on blood type alone. I obviously can't ask my dead wife who else she was sleeping with at the time Andi was conceived, but I need to know. I need to take measures to make sure no one ever shows up on my doorstep to try to take her away from me. She's *my* daughter. Do you hear me? No one else is ever going to lay claim to her, and I'm not going to live in fear. I need to know the truth."

Nick heard the low whistle at the other end of the phone. "So let me understand. You want me to find out who else your dead wife was sleeping with over eight years ago?"

"No. I want you to find out who impregnated her over eight years ago. Based on all the shit I've found since her death, you may find she was fucking an entire football team. I just need to know who is Andrea's biological father, and I need you to do it without raising their suspicion. For all I know, they have no idea Andi exists, and I want to keep it that way."

"Well, is that all? I thought you might have something hard for me."

"Listen, can you do the job or not?" Nick wasn't in the mood to deal with the PI's attempt at humor.

"Sure. I'm sorry. Email me with all the details you have. Your wife's name, DOB, social security number, and the same for your daughter. If you have a copy of the birth certificate, send it along with anything else you can think of that might help. I'll watch for it and be back in touch."

"Thanks."

"Don't thank me yet. You may not like what I dig up."

CHAPTER 11

*C*alista forced her voice to be strong despite the lump that kept forming in her throat. Andi needed her to be strong.

"You came back," the Beast said meekly. "At least I can see you this one time."

"No! No!" Belle said, sobbing as she kissed the Beast's cheek. "Please don't die... I love you."

At that moment the spell was broken, and in one magical instant, the Beast turned back into his princely self. The enchanted servants returned to their human forms as well. The castle came alive with rejoicing. Mrs. Potts cried human tears of joy as the handsome young prince gathered the beautiful Belle into his arms. Mrs. Potts, Cogsworth, and Lumiere had not one doubt that the loving couple would live happily ever after.

She was just closing the Disney storybook when she heard it, barely a whisper.

"Cali?"

Calista shot out of the chair to stand next to the bed. For the first time in two days, the eyes of the beautiful little girl she loved so much were open. Cali forced a comforting smile.

"Well, hello there, sleepyhead. I can't tell you how happy I am to see you awake."

"Where am I?" Her voice was scratchy from lack of use.

"You're in the hospital, sweetheart." Your Cali gently held her hand. "Your school bus was in an accident, but you're going to be just fine. The doctors and nurses have been taking really good care of you."

The confusion was easy to see on her innocent little face as Andi tried to remember. For her sake, Cali hoped she'd never recollect the accident clearly. Some things were best left forgotten—like visits to morgues in the middle of the night.

"Where's my dad? Is he still on his business trip?"

"Oh, of course not." Cali was relieved Andi's memory was intact. "He came rushing home the minute he heard about your accident. He's been here at the hospital the entire time since you were brought here. It's just bad luck he stepped out of the room for some coffee. He'll be back any minute."

"Who are you talking to, Cali? Are you done reading her *The Beauty and the Beast*?" His voice behind her startled Cali until she flushed with relief.

Cali winked at Andi as she leaned over her. Andrea seemed to understand. "She's done, Daddy. I was about to ask her to read *The Little Mermaid* next."

Nick was beside her in an instant. Cali moved aside to let him get closer to his daughter. Her heart melted, seeing his love for her shining in his eyes.

"Oh thank you, God. I've been so worried about you, Andi. How are you feeling?"

"Tired, I guess. My head hurts, and I'm really thirsty."

"You two catch up." Cali leaned down to place a soft kiss on Andi's forehead. "I'm gonna go let the nurse know you're awake." She squeezed Nick's forearm as she took her leave, and he looked up briefly. The relief of Andi waking up was sinking into his pained eyes. He didn't say a word—he didn't need to, Cali understood.

Calista stepped out into the hall but didn't go to the nurse's station immediately. She wanted to give Nick and Andi a few minutes to talk before alerting the nurse since she suspected they would be shooed out of the room so they could do some more tests now that their patient was awake.

As she expected, as soon as she alerted the nurse on duty, the RN picked up the phone to call Dr. Adams, then rushed into Andi's room. Nick came out a few minutes later, a look of relief finally overshadowing the exhaustion that had begun to take its toll on all of them.

He didn't say a word, just pulled Cali into his arms. They embraced for several long moments, each saying their thanks for Andrea waking up and appearing as if she was on the mend. They both knew she'd have a long recovery, but they were ready for it.

Before they could speak, Nick's cell phone rang. He pulled out of their hug to check the caller ID. "I'm sorry, but I need to take this call."

She watched him answer the phone as he walked away from the ICU and down the long hallway. It wasn't the first time Cali felt the weight of something she couldn't quite put her finger on.

Nick had been making and receiving too many mysterious calls in the two days they'd been camped out at the hospital together. At first, she'd been angry Nick thought work was so important, that he would need to keep working while his daughter was on her deathbed. Cali had eventually realized the calls he was taking were not business related which only made Cali more uncomfortable.

They hadn't talked about Dr. Adam's revelations

regarding Nick's blood type on the day of the accident. In part, Cali didn't have a clue what she could say that would make it better, but it was more than that. Like Nick, she just wanted to forget the terrible words. For both Nick and Andi's sake, she just wanted to sweep the whole revelation under the rug. After all, Roni was dead. No one else but Nick and Cali ever needed to know Nick was not Andi's biological father.

"What the hell are you saying? Babies don't just fall out of the sky." Nick had stepped outside the hospital into the spring sunshine that was a lot brighter than he felt. He should be enjoying the good news of Andi's improved condition, not getting more bad news.

"Listen, I'm just telling you what I've found so far. I tried to tell you yesterday you'd better be sure you wanted to open up this particular can of worms because there's no telling what you're gonna find. You already know your wife lied to you about a lot of important things in your marriage. Is this really such a surprise to you?"

"Yes, dammit. When she showed up with the baby, she'd gained a lot of weight like she'd just given birth. She made a big deal about how upset she was when she had to quit breastfeeding because Andrea wasn't getting enough nutrients according to the pediatrician. We didn't have sex for like three months until her OBGYN gave her the green light to start again after the baby was born."

"Did you actually see the baby breastfeeding?"

He racked his brains. Blackburn had to be wrong.

"Fuck, no."

"Did you go to the OBGYN with her for her checkups?"

"No."

"Did you ever notice any stretch marks on her? My ex-wife is full of them."

"Dammit. I swear to God, I wish I could bring her back to life just so I could kill her with my bare hands."

"I understand, but that isn't going to help."

Nick had only just begun to get his mind wrapped around the fact Veronica had deceived him about being Andi's father. There'd been a small part of him that held out hope it was just a big mistake or at the least, she too had believed Andi was his since they looked so much alike. Now, to find out Veronica herself had never given birth to a baby put a nail in her coffin. His PI had received a copy of the autopsy report and that, combined with other medical records, had confirmed Andrea was not the biological daughter of either Nick or Roni.

But where the hell had she come from and more importantly, how long until some stranger showed up on his doorstep wanting to steal his only daughter away from him?

"Let me keep digging. The trail isn't cold yet. I just wanted to fill you in with the newest information. I'm glad to hear Andrea is awake. Let me worry about this shit. You go back in and take care of your daughter. And Nick? She is your daughter in every way that counts."

The private investigator hung up without saying goodbye. It was just as well, Nick had no words for this situation. He sat on a bench in the small garden just outside the hospital entrance, trying to sort through the rush of emotions the most recent news evoked. He was lost in thought and missed Calista coming out looking for him until she took a seat next to him. They sat in silence for several minutes, watching people coming and going out of the building.

Cali broke the awkward silence. "When are you going to tell me what's going on, Nick?"

"Nothing's going on." He couldn't bear the thought of telling anyone, not even Calista, what he knew. He couldn't risk it.

"Really? Seriously, if you don't want to talk to me about it, do me a favor and just say so, but don't lie to me. I expected Kevin to lie, but not you."

"I'm sorry, Cali." He hated the pain in her voice, especially knowing he was responsible for it. "You're right. I don't want to hurt you, but I have a lot of shit on my plate right now." He wasn't prepared for her anger as she turned on the bench to glare at him.

"And I don't? I thought we were in this together. I thought we were becoming a team."

Nick's heart rate spiked. He didn't want to lose Cali, but he didn't have time to balance a new relationship right now when his life was literally falling apart.

"We are a team, but there are still a few things I'm gonna have to deal with on my own."

"Let me in. I know this is about what the doctor told you. We haven't talked about it, but now that Andi is awake, I think we should."

"There's nothing to talk about. He was mistaken. Andrea is my daughter in every sense of the word. Period."

He heard her emotional sigh. "Of course she is. Still, you must be a bit freaked out. Talk to me."

"There's nothing to talk about."

Her emotions turned to anger as she sprang to her feet.

"There you go, lying to me again. I can't believe I thought you were different, but you're not. I've got a newsflash for you. Your daughter just woke up from a coma and instead of sitting in there talking to her... comforting her, you're sneaking outside to take yet another private call. You don't want to level with me? That's fine, I'll leave. But you need to get your ass back in there and sit with her. She's afraid and asking for her daddy." Calista had turned and was already ten feet away when he came to his senses.

"Calista, don't go! Please."

She stopped, but she didn't turn around. Nick pushed to his feet to go to her. Cali refused to turn and look at him, so he hugged her from behind, holding onto her, trying to prevent her from leaving. He didn't want to lose Cali. Not over this... not ever. But could he trust her enough to tell her the truth? She already knew enough information to compromise him should word ever get out. Should he trust her with more? He was glad he couldn't see her eyes.

"I've hired a private detective. I need to know the truth. I need to know how to protect myself and Andrea from having someone show up in our lives to try to take her away from me. I can survive losing Roni, but I know for a fact, I wouldn't survive losing Andi. She's a part of me—whether she has my blood or not doesn't matter. She's my little girl. Do you understand what I'm saying?"

Cali turned in his arms, hugging his waist as she looked up into his eyes. He was relieved to see her anger had dissipated.

"I understand perfectly, Nick. Your secret is safe with me. I would never do anything to endanger you or Andrea."

He knew she spoke the truth. It helped him tell her everything.

"The PI I hired has uncovered that not only am I not Andrea's biological father, but... Veronica never gave birth."

Cali looked as confused as he felt. "But... how?"

"Who the hell knows? I feel like a complete idiot. I mean how the hell could she have lied about something like thi,s and I never figured it out?"

"She was a good actress. And this at least explains a few things."

"Like what?"

"Like why she and Andi never really bonded. You told me she would never win a mother-of-the-year award, but maybe it was deeper. I don't think she ever wanted to be a mother. Not really. I think Andi was just a way to trap you into marrying her. Didn't you say you had broken up with her before she showed up with the baby?"

"Fuck. You're right. In fact, the more I think about it, I bet that's why it was getting worse these last few years. The older Andi got, the more jealous Roni became of the time I'd spend with her."

"I bet it killed her to see you loving Andi so much, knowing the truth and never being able to tell you."

"I hope she is rotting in hell."

"I agree, and I understand you want to know the truth, so you can protect yourself and Andrea, but please, don't let it consume you or distract you from what's important. If no one has come looking for her by now, chances are very good they never will. You have to have faith."

At that moment, Nick knew how very lucky he was to have Cali in his life. He felt one hundred times better than he had even fifteen minutes before.

"Let's go see my daughter, shall we?"

CHAPTER 12

"All right, young lady. Let's get you in the house and up to your bed."

Cali was as relieved as Nick to be bringing Andrea home from the hospital. It had been a long week of recovery since she'd come out of the coma, but they'd finally received the green light from Dr. Adams to bring her home. It would still be another week before she could even think about going back to school. Cali had used her connections with her father-in-law to pressure the firm into giving Nick an extended leave of absence to take care of his daughter.

Andrea had other ideas about her recovery.

"But Dad, can't I lay down on the couch in the living room so I can watch movies with you and Cali?"

"Maybe tomorrow I'll carry you down, but today you're going right to bed."

"I've been in bed for over a week!"

"And you'll be in bed for another week if that's what it takes to get you back healthy. You heard Dr. Adams. We need to limit your TV and no video games."

They were just coming into the house through the garage. Nick scooped Andi up into his arms as she squealed with delight.

"I'm going to start some supper," Cali called after them as they headed up the stairs

"I want pizza!" Andi called back down to her.

Calista could hear Nick telling her she'd be eating soup and crackers. Her heart contracted with love as she listened to their playful banter. At times like this, she almost couldn't believe how happy she was with her new life. As horrific as the accidents had been, there was no denying they'd brought Nick and Cali to better places in their lives. She'd send Kevin and Roni thank you notes if she could.

Nick hadn't come down from Andi's room yet when the doorbell rang. Cali dried her hands and went to answer it. When she opened the door, she found a man she'd never seen before. Alarm bells started going off. They still hadn't gotten any more details on Andrea's paternity testing, and it was the one thing hanging out there that threatened to ruin their new lives together.

"Can I help you?"

"I'm looking for Nicholas Mikos."

"May I ask who's calling?"

The visitor hesitated long enough that Nick was halfway down the stairs.

"Did I hear the doorbell?"

Cali stepped back and opened the door wider so Nick could see their visitor as she answered, "Yes, I was just trying to understand how I might help this gentleman."

"Blackburn. What are you doing here? I was expecting you to call earlier."

"I decided I needed to see you in person. Can I come in?"

The look on Nick's face told Cali all she needed to know.

This was the private investigator, and he was here with more news. For a minute, she wondered if Nick was going to turn him away.

"Come on in. Cali was just making some soup and sandwiches. Would you like some coffee or a beer?"

The man named Blackburn followed Nick to the back of the house while Cali closed the door. She wasn't sure if she was supposed to follow them or not. Nick sensed her dilemma and turned to hold out his hand.

"Coming, baby?"

Relief flowed through her—he was letting her in on one of the most private conversations he might ever have. A conversation that could determine how much danger he was in of losing his daughter.

When they got to the kitchen, Cali went back to fixing dinner, trying not to hover over the men although it was clear she would hear everything that was discussed.

Blackburn didn't beat around the bush. He and Nick were only seated at the kitchen island for a few seconds before he asked an uncomfortable question.

"Are you sure you don't want to go to your office or somewhere more private for this conversation?"

Cali couldn't resist turning around. Nick looked at her with a loving smile before answering.

"I'm sure. Cali knows everything. I trust her."

"Okay, good enough for me." Blackburn launched into the reason for the visit. "So how much do you know about Veronica's work history between college and showing up with the baby?"

"She'd started out in nursing which was a joke considering she hated the sight of blood. She switched her degree over to healthcare administration. I know she had a couple of different jobs working in doctors' offices when we were dating, then I think she got a position in admissions at some hospital at one point, right before we broke up."

"Exactly. I'm almost certain that's where she had access to infants."

Nick jumped up to his feet. "Jesus Christ. Are you telling me she stole a baby? She was a conniving bitch, but I don't believe she'd outright steal someone's baby."

"Sit down. Let me finish." Once Nick sat, Blackburn continued. "There were no babies reported stolen or missing from Baltimore Memorial during the time she worked there, but I did some digging into all the births during the three-month period around Andi's birthday just the same, trying to track down where all of those babies were today and found a couple of interesting things."

Cali had just turned to start dinner when she heard Baltimore Memorial. Her pulse picked up at just the mention of a place that had brought her so much pain in her youth. Unwanted memories invaded of a year that had changed her life forever. She had fought so hard to forgive and forget, but in the end, her family had fallen apart forever in that damn hospital.

She hadn't been paying attention for a while, so when she started listening again, she had trouble following the conversation. Blackburn seemed to be going through a list of names.

"Not only was the guy I talked to at the address on the admissions record acting funny, but that was the only name on the list that was definitely of Greek heritage. You sent me Andrea's picture, and it's clear to me that was how Veronica was so successful in her ruse. Andrea looks so much like you, and I'm guessing her parents were Greek as well. As you know, there's a large Greektown in Baltimore. I'm heading back down there tomorrow to take another crack at the guy in person, this time to see if I can find out more."

Cali's heart was pounding so hard, her ears were ringing. The room had started to spin, and she vaguely heard Nick cautioning Blackburn to be careful, the last thing they needed was to get someone suspicious of why they were asking questions.

"When is Andi's birthday?" Cali blurted the question, interrupting the men. "I know it was recently."

Nick looked confused as to why she was interrupting with a stray question, yet he answered. "February."

Her breaths were becoming shorter. It couldn't be? They wouldn't have done that to her?

"When in February?"

"Why?"

"Nick, just tell me! What day is her birthday?" She hadn't meant to shout at him.

"Valentine's Day. She was born on Valentine's Day in 2007."

"Holy fuck." Cali almost collapsed. Nick jumped up to rush to her, catching her in time, helping her to sit on an open stool at the island.

"Calista, you're scaring me. What's wrong, baby?"

"It's not possible. Every single year... they knew how brokenhearted I was. They wouldn't have..."

"You're not making sense."

Cali knew the next question she needed to ask, it came out as a whisper.

"Who are you going to see tomorrow in Baltimore?"

Blackburn looked down at the open file on the counter before looking up with his answer. "George Petros."

She heard the howl of pain. It took her a few seconds to realize it was coming from her. She sensed Nick holding her up, keeping her from falling and could see the worry etched on his face. It was the last thing she saw before she fainted into his arms.

Something was terribly wrong, Nick just couldn't figure out what it was. After Cali fainted, he scooped her into his arms and carried her to the living room couch to lay her down.

"Blackburn, will you wet a couple paper towels with some cold water and bring them over?" The PI didn't answer, but Nick could see him moving into action in the kitchen.

He looked down on Calista's pale face, not understanding what had happened that upset her. He replayed the conversation they'd been having over in his head and came up without an answer.

He placed a pillow under her head and propped up her feet. When the cold compresses arrived, he started wiping her face until she started coming around. She awoke in the same panic as when she had fainted. Her eyes looked frantic, and it cut him.

"Shhh. Calista, you're safe. Take a few deep breaths, baby." Blackburn pushed a glass of cold water into his hand, and Nick lifted it to her lips and helped her to take a few sips.

"You have to believe me, Nick. I swear to you. I'm not like Veronica. They lied to me too. I didn't know." Her panic wasn't receding.

"Slow down, Cali. I know you are nothing like Veronica. Now, who lied to you?"

Her answer was in the form of an anguished cry. "My parents."

She hadn't wanted to talk about her family with him. All Nick knew was her mom had died when she was in college, and she was estranged from her dad. She was an only child.

"What did they lie about?" Nick was confused. She shook her head as if she was afraid to answer. Blackburn stepped up closer to peer down on them from above as he pushed her for answers.

"What did they lie about, Calista?"

"Why did they do this to me?" She looked between the men frantically. "Year after year, they watched me go to her grave and put flowers there. The whole time they knew where she was. They let it tear us apart and didn't stop it."

"Cali, you're not making sense." Nick was more confused than ever, but Blackburn seemed to be catching on.

"What was your maiden name, Ms. Bennett?"

Cali didn't answer. She was falling apart before their eyes.

"All this time. I lost so much time." She looked like she was going into shock. Nick played Blackburn's last question over in his mind. Why would he be asking for her maiden name?

"Daddy, what's wrong with Cali?" Nick looked over the back of the couch to see Andi in her pajamas. She couldn't be here.

"You aren't supposed to be out of bed, Andi. Go on. Up to bed. I'll bring your dinner to you soon."

She wasn't listening to him, she was too worried about Cali. Cali was pushing to sit up all of a sudden as Andi came around to stand near them.

The frantic look in her eyes as she looked at Andi scared him, yet as each second passed, Calista seemed to calm more until her breathing had normalized. When she reached for his hand, he could feel her trembling.

"I never told you why I didn't want to go back to Greece."

"Is that really important right now?"

"Yes. Unfortunately, it is." She gave a sad smile. "I spent several summers in Greece with my dad's family. My mom and dad usually went with me, but when I was fifteen, my parents let me go by myself. I felt so grown up to be traveling alone. It was different being there without them though. I didn't speak enough Greek, so I just hung out with my cousin." The panic was returning to her beautiful face. "I swear to you, Nick, I didn't know."

"Didn't know what?"

Cali tore her gaze away from his to look down at their joined hands. It was as if she couldn't look him in the eye and it made him uncomfortable. He almost missed her answer.

"Angelo."

"Who's Angelo?"

"My cousin. He was two years older than me... and... he liked me."

Nick's mind was racing with what she was trying to tell him. It couldn't be.

"He liked me a lot, but he... hurt me... bad." Her eyes met his again, the tears flowing freely down her cheeks. "My grandfather disowned him and shipped me home right away, but it was too late. My parents were furious I'd been hurt in Greece, and it caused major family problems. By the time I found out I was..." She stopped to look at Andi with a look of love that melted his heart before returning her gaze to Nick. "...that I was pregnant, it was already too late for... well you know. I wouldn't have done it, anyway. Never. I knew I was too young to be a mother, but it didn't matter to me. My parents fought about it constantly, but I told them it was my decision."

It was Nick's turn to look at his daughter. When he turned back to Cali, all he could say was, "Impossible."

Calista looked up at Blackburn. "February 14, 2007?"

"Yes."

"Baltimore Memorial?"

"Yes."

"Mother's name Olympia Petros?"

He looked at the file in his hands before answering, "Yes."

"But who is Olympia Petros?" Nick injected,

"Olympia was my great-grandma's name. My parents named me after her." She reached across to her purse on the nearby end table. She pulled out her passport and handed it to Nick. His hands were shaking as he opened it to see Olympia Calista Petros. "I had to use this as ID recently when filling out paperwork at the bank. I haven't updated my passport yet with Bennett, and now I never will."

They all sat in silence for a long minute before Andi asked, confused.

"Daddy, what does this mean?"

He saw the hope in Cali's eyes. For the first time, he looked back and forth between the two most important women in his life, really seeing each of them and their resemblance—the black hair, amber-brown eyes. At that moment, Nick accepted that surely, God had a hand in bringing them together. There could be no other explanation for the miracle of them finding each other.

"Daddy?"

Nick pulled Andi into his arms, so they were facing Cali on the couch.

"Andi, it means that Calista is your new mommy. Calista Petros Bennett, will you marry me?"

Cali's eye's opened wide with surprise. "Nick, you don't have to do this."

"Yes, Cali, I do."

"But you don't. You know I would never in a million years take her from you. You love her with all your heart."

"Yes, I do. But, I love her mother with all my heart too. Don't you see, Cali? We were meant to be a family. You just weren't ready back then, so I got an early start, but you're ready now. Think about it. There's no other explanation for us finding each other like this."

They all sat in stunned silence before Cali finally spoke.

"You're right. Just think, we never would have known if Kevin and Roni hadn't..." She thankfully cut off before she gave away too much in front of Andrea.

Nick knew exactly what she had been about to say.

"I know. God had to bless their betrayal."

CHAPTER 13

"*A*re you sure you want to go through with this?"

Cali heard the quaver of concern in Nick's voice as he pulled the car into the entrance of their destination. With Andrea reading in the back seat, they'd had to be careful what they said in the one hour drive up to Baltimore. It didn't matter. They'd talked of nothing else for the last twenty-four hours.

As miraculous as the news of their unexpected reunion was, Cali was absolutely sure she wouldn't find peace until she paid a difficult visit to her pained past. Only then would the new family of three be free to move forward with their lives together.

"I'm positive."

Nick didn't take his eyes off the winding gravel path he'd turned onto, letting the tree-lined private road weave them through stately rows of headstones to the secluded haven at the back of the cemetery. It was a place Cali had spent many hours in the past.

She used to come often, first to visit what she now knew to be the empty grave of her lost baby girl and later to pay respects to her mother. She had cried more tears in this peaceful haven than she cared to admit.

In the two weeks that had passed since she'd learned the shocking truth of her daughter's existence, Cali's emotions had run the gamut, fluctuating wildly between grateful awe at the miracle of it all and blinding anger, usually aimed at her parents. Since her mother was already dead, her father took the brunt of her anger.

How could he have done this to her? She just couldn't fathom how he'd looked at her, spoken to her... hell, watched her bring flowers and cry over what he knew to be an empty grave. All the while, he'd remained silent.

Well, today, he would be giving her answers. Today, he would no longer be able to hide behind his bold-faced lies.

Nick pulled the family van to a stop several hundred feet before the final bend in the drive that would lead to the Petros family plots. She'd drawn a rudimentary map for him the night before after filling him in on her plan for the next day. He'd done his best to dissuade her from putting herself through the emotional upheaval this meeting would bring, but Cali couldn't bring herself to call it off.

She needed answers, and there was only one person alive who had them.

Once parked, Nick finally turned to face Cali, worry etched on his face.

"At least let me go with you," he begged.

She was already shaking her head. "I need to do this alone."

"I don't like this."

Hearing the love and concern in his voice helped Cali soften her reply. "I know, and I really am sorry for that. I honestly don't know what to expect, but I just know I have to confront him on my own."

"You promise to text me the second you need me, right?"

"I promise." Patting her pocket, she confirmed she'd brought her cell phone.

Cali's right hand was on the door handle when Nick grabbed her left hand, holding her in the vehicle until she turned back to face him.

"Remember how much we love you and..." he paused, looking pained before bravely adding the words they had fought over the night before. "We wouldn't have met if he hadn't done what he did."

She saw the sadness in his eyes and knew her continued anger at her father for robbing her of eight years with her daughter hurt her fiancé deeply. They were both so raw from the events of the previous months.

Nick couldn't help feeling grateful for her parent's deception any more than she could help her anger at their betrayal. She knew she was walking a tightrope of emotions, furious at her lost time and yet so grateful that God had brought their family together.

Intellectually, she knew Nick was right. She hadn't been ready to be a mother at sixteen. She probably wouldn't have gone to college. She wouldn't have met Kevin, and therefore, she would have almost certainly never met Nick, the man she loved with all of her heart. He was a good and honorable man—a fabulous father—a fantastic lover.

They were truly blessed.

So why couldn't she just let her parents' deception go and move on to live her new fairytale life?

Cali finally squeezed Nick's hand back, trying to reassure him. "I love you too, and I really am so grateful we're a family now. I don't know how I know, but I just won't be able to move on until I confront him. Please... try to understand."

"I do understand. I just don't want you to open old wounds. I want to be the one who helps you heal."

Cali leaned across the center console to plant a quick kiss

on Nick's sexy lips. He took advantage of her proximity to pull her closer.

"Believe it or not, this is part of the healing process for me, Nick. I need answers before I can close this part of our story."

He caught her lips in one more quick kiss before pulling back, signaling he'd finally watch her leave for her meeting with her father. He'd be parked far enough away, he wouldn't be able to hear the resulting confrontation, but he'd be close enough to swoop in and help her if she needed him.

And for that she was grateful.

A cool spring breeze met her as she exited the van. There was a storm forming in the west, matching her mood perfectly. Cali pulled the cardigan she'd worn around her tighter, hugging her middle, self-consciously trying to hold it together long enough to get answers she so desperately needed.

As she rounded the final curve in the path through the stately graveyard, she saw her father was already waiting for her at their arranged meeting place. Her footsteps faltered. She arrived twenty minutes early intentionally, wanting the time at her mother's grave to gather her final thoughts before confronting her remaining parent.

As if sensing her arrival, her father looked up to see her approaching. Even at a distance, she could see the tears on his ruddy cheeks. Calista proceeded slowly, in part to gather her thoughts but more because the stark vision of a man who was a mere shell of his former self alarmed her.

As she approached, George Petros pulled a hankie from his coat jacket to blow his nose, ironically attempting to hide his tears from his daughter. If he could have read her mind, he'd left the tears visible. They did more to soften Calista's anger than any words he might choose to say in their upcoming confrontation.

"Father." It was the only salutation she could muster as she came to a halt a few feet from him.

"Hello, my Olympia."

Long gone were the 'daddies' and 'Cali's' from her youth. Those familiar terms of endearment had been absent from their strained relationship since the heated disagreements eight years before had set them on the bumpy path they found themselves on today. She found it ironic that now when she had more reason to be angry at him than before, she missed her daddy more than ever.

They stood in awkward silence—Calista unsure of the right words to break open the wounds festering between them, her father not understanding why she'd called him to meet here of all places.

Cali glanced away, focusing instead on the two graves they stood in front of. It felt so different being here again, knowing now her baby's casket was empty. As angry as she was at the lost time, she took a moment to thank God for Andrea's life. Her anger softened as a rush of love and relief washed over her at realizing she now had an adorable, living face for the infant she'd mourned.

"I'm so very sorry, Calista." His voice broke with emotion, but his words sparked her anger anew.

Turning to him, she confronted her parent. "What is it, exactly, you're sorry for, Dad?"

Startled at her harsh tone, he looked up, alarm in his eyes. She waited for his shaky response. "For so many things."

They were in a stare down. Not ready to let him off the hook yet, she pressed him. "Name just one."

"I'm sorry I killed your mother."

His confession shook her. It was unexpected.

"Mom died of a heart attack. I hardly think that was your fault," she countered, confused at her own instinct to defend the man she was so angry with.

"Of course it was. She died of a broken heart. She couldn't forgive…" His words cut off abruptly.

"Forgive what?"

Her dad took a deep breath, choosing his words carefully. "Not what. Who." He paused long enough she wondered if he'd finish his reply. When he continued, it was a mere whisper. "She couldn't forgive me for driving the wedge between you and us."

"It's a bit more than a wedge. It's a damn cavern."

"Yes, I didn't handle your pregnancy well."

She scoffed. "You think? You treated me like I embarrassed you. Like you were ashamed of me!"

"No! I was never ashamed of you, Calista. Never," he defended.

"You could have fooled me! You refused to let me go to school once I started showing. We stopped going to church. Hell, the last two months, I didn't leave the house even once, not until it was time to go to the hospital. Those aren't the actions of someone who wasn't ashamed." She'd raised her voice until she ended in a shout. Her parent responded in kind.

"Of course I was ashamed but not of you! Of myself, for failing to protect you. Of my family. It was my nephew who hurt you. I should have been there! Your grandparents… my brother… so many people I trusted failed you."

He'd never said those words before.

"Dad, only Angelo was responsible for his actions."

"No! There's plenty of blame to go around. And yes, I was furious, but at the men in my family, not you, Calista. Never you."

"Forgive me, but it sure as hell didn't seem like it back then. You barely spoke to me after I got home. The only time you talked to me was to remind me I had to hide the pregnancy as if it were a curse."

"Of course it was a curse! You were fifteen, barely sixteen, when you delivered. You were still a child yourself."

Knowing the perfection that was Andrea, she couldn't let his comment stand. "That innocent baby was never a curse. She was perfect!"

Fresh tears sprang to his eyes as he finally broke their visual connection to look away towards the dark clouds rolling closer. Thunder rumbled in the distance, matching the storm brewing between them.

"She was perfect. You're right about that," he answered finally.

Cali stepped closer, grabbing his forearm through his coat as she asked the question burning between them. "How could you do it, Father?" she accused.

When he looked back at her, she saw the panic in his eyes. Still, he wasn't ready to acknowledge his deepest sin.

"I don't know…"

"Stop! Enough lies. I came here today for the truth. Finally, the truth."

His fear was palpable. She glared at him until he finally answered.

"I knew that damn private detective showing up with questions was the beginning of the end."

His words were ironic because to Calista, the truth wasn't the end. On the contrary, it felt like her life had really just begun. Still, she wasn't ready to let him off the hook yet.

"How could you watch me come here, again and again, knowing her grave was empty?"

He flinched, recognizing she did indeed know his most shameful secret.

"It broke my heart to see you in pain."

"Pain you caused. Why?"

"I did it for you. Don't you see? You were too young."

"That wasn't your decision! It was my life."

"I did what I thought was best for you. I wanted you to have choices. College. A career. Marriage. Other children."

"And how did that work out, Dad? Here I am with a dead husband. No new baby."

His tears were back. "I know, Calista. And I never dreamed I'd lose both you and your mother over my choice that day. She never forgave me, you know. The stress of hiding the lie we couldn't undo and watching your pain refusing to fade, it drove her to this very grave."

Until that moment, Cali had placed the blame for their deception on her parents equally. They had both been vocal about their wanting her to put her baby up for adoption. In the weeks since she'd found out Andrea was alive, she'd assumed her parents had shared the blame equally for their lies.

"I need answers."

"Cali…"

"No, I *deserve* answers. Babies don't just disappear out of hospitals without their mother's knowing what happened to them. For now, forget about the *why*. I need to know *how* you did it."

The older man's face fell. "I'll tell you anything you want to know, but we can't separate the how and the why. Even now, knowing what it would cost me, I'm not sure I could have chosen anything different on that day."

"How can you possibly say that? You lost your whole family that day with that one decision!"

"Yes." He swayed on his feet, and for a moment, she thought he might topple over. Cali resisted the urge to reach out to steady him.

His tone changed as if he were reading from an old storybook from the past. "I was sitting in the waiting room while your mother went into the delivery room with you. We'd been at the hospital for over twelve hours, at that point, I guess. You'd been in such pain, and I sat in that damn room, so angry at Angelo and my family... angry at myself, for failing you. Wishing I could just go back in time and keep you home the summer before."

Cali had to bite her tongue to keep from interrupting him. She gave him time to continue.

"I'd been out there waiting about an hour I guess when the young woman who'd checked us in at admissions when we'd arrived came into the waiting room. She addressed me by name and told me to follow her. She said she had an update for me on your condition.

"I so terrified something bad had happened, I would have followed her anywhere to get answers. We wound away from the maternity ward, through the emergency room entrance, finally ending at the small chapel in the middle of the hospital. As soon as we went in, I started crying because I was just sure she'd brought me there to break the news to me that you'd died in childbirth."

"That's crazy! Mom would have come out to tell you if there'd been a problem like that."

"Believe me. I've replayed that day over in my head a thousand times, and I know that now, but at the time, all I could think about was my baby was in pain."

It felt odd having her father call her his baby. She hadn't felt like his baby in a very long time.

"Anyway, the young woman introduced herself, but I was so upset I missed all the details. All I remember hearing her say was she could see what a great father I was—how worried I looked for your wellbeing. She commented about how hard it must be to watch my sixteen-year-old, unwed daughter giving birth.

"When I figured out she didn't have any update on your delivery, I got angry. I turned to leave, but that was when she called out she might have a solution to my problem."

"My baby wasn't a problem!"

"Yes, Calista it was."

"*She*, Dad. My baby wasn't an *it*. She was a perfect baby girl."

"I didn't mean…"

"Yes, you did. That was your biggest mistake. You never saw her as a living, breathing part of me. You only saw her as this sin. But I carried her inside me. I felt her moving. I sang songs to her and read her books. I felt every hiccup… every kick. She was alive, and she was part of *me*, not just Angelo. And when you let me believe she had died, a part of me died too."

Her words stunned him into silence, so she continued.

"To you, I was your baby, but don't you see? She was *my* baby. *Mine*. You didn't have the right to take her away from me."

New tears streamed down his face as he finally apologized. "I'm so sorry, Calista. If only I could go back and walk out the door of that chapel, I would. Maybe then your mother would be here with us, and I wouldn't have to tell you how sorry I am you'll never know your daughter."

For the first time that day, Calista felt her own pang of guilt. This time, she was the one with the power to relieve his grief, but she wasn't prepared to let him off the hook. Not yet.

"What could that woman possibly say to you that could convince you to break my heart? How much did she pay you?"

"Nothing! I didn't sell my granddaughter! I really did think I was giving her a better life. A life you weren't in a position to give her."

"That's such a load of crap."

"Is it? You were a sophomore in high school. How would you care for a baby and finish your schooling? And what about college? Marriage? This woman and her husband had been trying for several years to have a child. They'd prayed for a baby. He had a good job. They owned a house. They would love your little girl."

"And you just believed her? What if she lied to you?" Cali had the advantage of knowing Veronica had lied. She'd played her father to secure her own future with Nick. The baby had merely been a means to an end for her.

"I didn't believe her at first. I was ready to walk out. To rush back to try to get an update on you, but that's when it happened." He cut off abruptly. His expression changed to an unreadable glare. He glanced away, looking up at the sky and then down at his wife's grave.

Cali had to prod him on. "What happened?"

He refused to look back at her. "You won't believe me. Your mother never did. It's why she couldn't forgive me."

"What? Just spit it out! I deserve answers. What could have possibly happened that would make you just give away my baby without talking to me about it first?"

He took a deep, shuddering breath as if he were steeling himself to say hard words.

"So much time has passed. I've wondered myself if I'd imagined it. If maybe in my desperation to find a solution to getting you your old life back, I'd dreamt the whole thing, but I know it happened. I know because when I get to my lowest points, I... well..." He paused before finally finishing, "I relive it in my dreams, over and over. In many ways, it's like it happened yesterday. Those dreams are the only thing that bring me comfort."

His veiled explanation was pissing her off. "What happened, Dad? Just spit it out."

A long moment passed before he answered with one confusing word.

"God."

For the first time that day, her father's face softened with a new peace hadn't been there before.

"God..." she repeated flatly. "What about God?"

Her parent lifted his gaze to hers and answered, "He was there. He told me to trust her."

Calista was a Christian. She'd prayed to God many times in her life for answers. If she were truthful, it was usually in anger. Anger for his taking her baby from her. Her mother from her. Even her cheating husband in the weeks right after Kevin's accident. She'd placed the blame on God at times in her darkest hours, but never... not once... had she gone so far as to voice her accusation as if he were in the room.

"Very funny. What really happened? And don't try to shift the blame onto someone who couldn't possibly be here to defend himself."

"You weren't there. It was..." he paused, searching for the right word and finally coming out with, "...miraculous."

"Enough! Stop with the nonsense..."

"Listen to me. I know it sounds crazy, but..." He was desperate, reaching out to latch onto her arms and tug her closer, refusing to let her leave.

"But what?"

"The chapel was dark. It was in the middle of the building. There were no windows. I glanced around when we arrived, and it was empty. The only light came from a few small sconces on the walls leaving the space in an eerie shadow. That was until..."

"Until what?" She had to prod him again.

"I'd turned from the altar and was walking back to the door. The young woman grabbed on to my arm and was begging me to listen to her. We were almost to the door when the room grew bright. Only it wasn't like someone had turned on the normal lights. It was more like... like someone was shining a spotlight on us from above, only we were in the middle of the building. There were many floors of hospital rooms above us. When I turned back towards the altar, all the candles were lit. I'm certain they hadn't been just minutes before because I remember thinking that maybe I should light a candle for you while I was there."

Calista was truly stunned by the length her father was going to in order to cover up his actions years before. He was many things, but she never dreamed he'd go to such lengths to come up with a crazy story to try to justify his actions.

"Do you hear how insane you sound? Do you honestly think I'm going to believe—"

Her father cut her off. "I swear to you, it happened. And that wasn't all. I'd entered that chapel panicked… depressed… worried. In the space of a few seconds, all that changed, and I felt a peace wash over me unlike any I've felt before or after."

"So, poof! God just showed up?"

Her father's fingers dug into her arm through her sweater. "I knew you wouldn't believe me, but I know what I felt. I may not have seen him, but I didn't need to see him to know he was there. It was like the magic on Christmas Eve, I could just feel him."

"You sound crazy, you know that?"

"I do know, but it doesn't matter. You asked for the truth, and I'm trying to give it to you. In those few minutes standing in that chapel, I saw a vision of you and your future family, and you looked so happy. There was another little girl with you. Your future daughter. And the man who was hugging both of you looked so happy. I don't know who he was, but I believe with all of my heart he's out there somewhere, waiting for you Calista.

"I was confused when you brought Kevin home a couple of years ago because he didn't look anything like the man in my vision. And he sure as hell never looked at you with the kind of love like in my dream, not even on your wedding day. It all puzzled me, but in the months since Kevin's death, the vision from that day has returned. Stronger. Clearer. It's how I know that something... *someone* better... is still out there. I know I can never get your daughter back, but I just have to believe you will find happiness. You'll get your family in the future."

Somewhere in the middle of her father's rambling story, the seed of awe she'd first felt the fateful day they'd discovered Andrea was indeed her biological daughter exploded inside her own chest, spilling a new warmth through her chilled body. As if to accentuate the moment, a bright flash of lightning lit the darkened sky before a loud crack of powerful thunder shook the ground under their feet.

Calista turned her father's words around in her head, letting them seep down to her heart, thawing her anger.

She and Nick had spent hours hashing through the events leading up to the fateful moment they'd met, searching for some logical explanation for how they'd been brought together. She suspected many, if not most, would call their meeting a coincidence. Maybe just good luck.

But in the quiet of the night as they'd clung to each other, she and Nick had both confessed their belief only God could have truly set such a complicated plan in motion years before. Still, it was one thing to admit her faith to Nick, the only other person alive directly impacted by the ruse Veronica and her parents had put into motion.

Now, to hear her father echo her own belief was surreal. That he'd felt a spiritual intervention even back on the day of his fateful decision rocked Cali to her core.

He broke through her thoughts. "I know. You think I'm crazy, just like your mother did. Oh, how I've wished she'd been there, too. My vision is the only thing that's brought me any comfort all of these years."

"So you really believe it then?" she asked, suddenly wanting more than anything to believe her father.

His gaze was steady, serene for the first time that day. "With every fiber of my being. I wish I knew when or how, but I just know there are a new man and a beautiful daughter in your future. And when you find them, you'll finally be happy again."

She'd come there angry, ready for a fight. At that moment, all fight left her as she accepted the future her father had seen for her had arrived. She had Nick and Andrea in her life. They'd made it through all the bullshit they needed to survive to get to this moment. It suddenly felt foolish to think of spending even a minute more of their precious time together being angry at the years she'd lost.

That was the truth Nick had been trying to convince her of for the last two weeks. They were always meant to be together, but there would have been no way for a twenty-six-year-old man to meet and be part of her life at sixteen. He'd been ready to become Andrea's father, to love her... protect her... take care of her in a way Cali couldn't have. At least, not back then.

She felt the first stray drop of rain as she pulled her cell phone from the pocket of her jeans, shooting off a quick text before stowing it away again. When she looked back at her parent, he seemed like he was holding his breath, waiting for his daughter's verdict if she would be cutting him out of her life once and for all for his betrayal.

Calista struggled to find the right words. Lingering anger stubbornly prevented her from giving him a total pass, but newfound understanding of the role her parent had reluctantly played in a higher plan for her life helped her feel the first seeds of forgiveness. She loved Nick too much to continue to begrudge him the years he'd spent with Andrea.

And maybe, just maybe, it might be time to let her father feel some of the same relief she now felt.

She knew the second Nick and Andrea came into sight behind her. She had the perfect view of her father's face as he looked off in the distance. As each second ticked by, his complexion paled as if he saw a ghost. Cali could see him trembling and reached out to hold his arms, helping to steady him.

"Impossible..." he whispered. The wind was picking up, and she struggled to hear the soft word.

"I'm beginning to think anything is possible, Dad."

By the time he looked back into her eyes, she could see a cocktail of relief and confusion warring in the older man's eyes. It was his turn to demand answers.

"How is this possible? Who are they?" he asked, pure awe in his voice.

She waited a few seconds until she saw Nick and Andi in her peripheral view. To his credit, her father kept his gaze on hers, waiting for her reply.

Calista released her dad's arm and reached out to her right. Nick moved them closer, sandwiching Andrea between them as they all faced her father.

"They are your family," she announced.

She finally tore her gaze away from her father's, and they both turned to look at Andrea and Nick, pride and love spilling out of her as she introduced them. "Dad, this is Nicholas Mikos, my fiancé, and this young lady is our daughter, Andrea."

It took her dad a few long seconds to internalize her words. When he did, he glanced between Calista, Nick, and Andi and back again.

Nick broke the awkward silence, stepping forward to offer his hand. "Hello, Mr. Petros. It's nice to finally meet you."

Her father was in shock. He clung to Nick's hand, refusing to release him as if he was afraid if he let go, Nick would disappear like the vision of him had years before.

"You have no idea how long I've waited to meet you, young man. And I can't thank you enough for putting a smile on my daughter's face. She's lived through so many trials already. I hope you'll allow her to adopt your daughter. She'll be the absolute best mother."

Nick glanced at Calista nervously, unsure how to respond to her father's comment.

Cali stepped forward, pulling Nick's hand free of the death grip her father had on it.

"Dad, I don't think you understand. Andi is already my daughter. I don't need to adopt her."

"But… of course you need to…" his voice trailed off. Her father turned back, this time taking a good look at Andrea for the first time. With each passing second, his eyes grew wider. "Impossible," he repeated.

"We thought so too, but it's true. Say hi to your papa, Andi."

Her eight-year-old daughter broke into a beautiful smile that had the power to chase away even the darkest of memories. She knew then the Petros family had spent their last day mourning lost time.

George Petros stepped forward, dropped to his knees, and pulled a surprised Andi into his arms. He clung to his granddaughter who graciously hugged him back. Tears clouded Cali's vision as she watched them cling to each other as several more fat raindrops fell from the darkening sky.

Calista's and Nick's eyes met over the heads of the hugging couple below, and she felt a new peace. The kind of serenity that can only be felt when all is right in the world. It was a calmness she hadn't truly felt since her innocent childhood had been stolen from her by her cousin halfway around the world. One act of violence had set them all on a crash course with fate.

She knew she had a choice. She could keep looking back, angry at all that she'd lost, or she could look forward to her future with the handsome man looking at her with a totally inappropriate sexy look on his face. Her heart fluttered, feeling wholly surrounded by Nick's love.

"It looks like we're about to get rained on. I think we should head home, don't you?" Nick asked.

Calista watched her father finally pull out of the death-grip he had on Andi. The vulnerable longing in his eyes as he looked at her cut her to the core.

Cali held her hand out to her father. Only after she'd helped pull him to his feet, did she add her invitation.

"How would you like to come to dinner tonight, Dad? I'd love to show you our new home. Andi can show you her princess bedroom."

It was Cali's turn to be pulled into a fatherly hug. "I've waited eight years for this invitation. Thank you, from the bottom of my heart."

As the raindrops fell harder, Andi latched onto her grand-father's hand and started pulling him along toward the cars. Over the wind, Cali could hear her asking him, "Cali says you grew up in Greece. Daddy wants to take us all on a family vacation there next summer. Maybe you can come with us and help be our tour guide."

Nick chuckled as they each wrapped an arm around the other to follow behind her dad and Andi.

"So that seemed to go better than you expected."

Cali snuggled against his body as they rushed towards the van, dodging raindrops as they went. The rain had started to come down harder just as they arrived at the van where Andi and her dad were waiting.

Nick unlocked the doors. "Why don't you just leave your

car here. I'll bring you back later to pick it up. You can ride with us," he invited.

As her father looked toward her to see if Cali minded, he broke into a huge grin.

"Look! If that isn't a sign, I don't know what is."

Confused, Cali, Nick and Andi turned to look where her father pointed. In the distance, a bright ray of sunshine shone through a small break in the rain clouds. The four of them stood in the sprinkles, enjoying nature's miracle until the rain grew stronger.

Nick still had his arm wrapped around her, making her feel safe and loved.

"Let's go home, baby."

She didn't tell him, but she was already home. Home would forever be where Nick and Andi were. She was truly blessed.

EPILOGUE

One Year Later:

"*That* was the best movie, ever! Can we stay and watch it again?"

Calista's heart expanded as she heard the excitement in her daughter's voice. She was trailing behind her family and watched the look of love on Nick's face as he hugged Andi close in the crowd pressing to exit the movie theater.

"I think once is enough for today. Maybe I'll bring you and Katie next weekend if you'd like to see it again."

As they walked out into the April sunshine, Cali debated asking Nick to get the car to pick her up at the front entrance. She didn't want to worry him, but she had barely been able to pay attention to the movie. She hadn't felt well all day and couldn't wait to get home and put her swollen feet up.

As the crowd dispersed, he was waiting to take her hand

with a concerned smile on his face. "You've been quiet. Are you feeling okay, baby?"

Calista didn't get a chance to answer before a tight cramping consumed her swollen abdomen. She had to stop walking to bend over in pain, squeezing Nick's hand as hard as she could while she rode out the sharp pain. Gratefully, it passed a minute later, leaving her feeling drained and out of breath.

"Oh my God, are you in labor?"

Calista righted herself but leaned heavily on her husband. "Well, I didn't think so before now, but that sure felt like a contraction."

"Mommy, are you okay? What's wrong?" Cali heard the panic in Andi's voice as she pressed closer, and Cali hugged her.

"I'm just fine, but I think it's almost time for you to become a big sister. It feels like your brother or sister was not happy they missed the movie and is trying to join us in time to see it with you next weekend."

Nick's face was pale. "But it's two weeks early."

"Don't panic. Dr. Galloway told me it could be anytime when I saw him yesterday."

"And you're just telling me this now? We should have stayed home today. You should be in bed. You should be..."

"Shhh." Cali cut him off with two fingers to his lips. "I'm pregnant, Nick, not sick. Everything is going to be fine."

She sounded stronger than she felt. Inside she was freaking out at the thought of giving birth again, but since she couldn't wait to hold her and Nick's baby in her arms, she steeled herself for the painful labor ahead. Nick, on the other hand, was falling apart.

"What should we do? Should we call the doctor? Should we go straight to the hospital?"

Before she could answer they should go home and wait

until the pains got closer together, the next contraction consumed her. A burning pain gripped her lower abdomen and spread up her spine.

Cali made it through the wave of pain by squeezing Andi with her left hand and Nick's hand with her right. As other families around them filed out of the theater, they stood linked, waiting for the arrival of the newest member to their family.

When the contraction ended, Cali smiled weakly. "I think the hospital sounds like a good idea."

Nick scooped her into his arms and carried her to the family van. He helped her recline in the back with Andi while he drove too fast to the hospital. He called Katie's parents from his Bluetooth on the drive. They had arranged for Andi to stay with her best friend when it was time for the birth. Unfortunately, they were an hour away, so it would be some time before they would arrive to pick up Andi.

"But Dad, I don't want to go to Katie's! I want to stay with you and Mommy." Her voice quavered with worry. Cali reached for Andi's hand.

"Honey, trust me. You'll be better over at Katie's until after the baby is born. It could take hours, and we can't leave you in the waiting room alone."

"But I'll come into your room with you. Please."

Before she could answer, the next contraction consumed Cali's attention. A wave of nausea had her fighting back the urge to throw up just as she felt wetness in her underwear, spreading quickly to her stretchy yoga pants and onto the seat. It felt like her body was exploding. She was relieved to see Nick run a red light to get her to the hospital as quickly as possible.

By the time they arrived at the emergency room, Calista knew the wetness between her legs was from her water breaking. For the last ten minutes, she'd felt as if she had sprung a slow leak that she couldn't possibly stop even if she wanted to. While Nick ran in to get a nurse and a wheelchair, Andi held her mom's hand tightly, afraid to let go.

"Andi, honey. I know we read the book together on where babies come from. Everything that's happening is completely normal. You're going to be a big sister very soon."

"I don't ever want to be a mommy. Not if it hurts this bad."

"Oh, you don't mean that. Having you here with me is worth every single pain I had."

They had tried to explain to Andrea the complicated circumstances of her birth as best as they could with an eight, now nine-year-old. She was an intelligent little girl and accepted the truth of her parentage with an ease Cali and Nick marveled at.

"Did it hurt when you had me, too?"

Calista's answer was delayed by another strong contraction that brought grunts of pain. She answered meekly as she saw Nick running out the door of the ER.

"Of course it hurt, and it took a long time since it was my first time, but what hurt the worst was when I thought you had died. That broke my heart."

Andrea's face lit up. "But now I'm your little miracle, right?"

"You bet you are. Finding you and your daddy was the best thing that ever happened to me, Andrea."

Time passed in a blur for Calista as she was rushed into an ER examination room before quickly being transferred up to the maternity ward after the nurse's examination discovered she was already at nine centimeters and moving quickly through labor. Apparently, it was true second births progress much quicker than the first.

Cali fought hard to hold back from screaming as the burning pain consumed her. Not one part of her body was left out of the party. The strain of the baby pressing to evacuate her womb was intense. She wanted to push so bad, but the nurses were all cautioning her to hold off until the doctor arrived.

Nick and Andrea sat next to her, each holding her hand. Nick wiped a cold washcloth across her forehead, worry etched on his handsome face. Surprisingly, Andrea appeared calmer as the birth approached. She watched the OB nurses carefully, taking in the excitement of the event.

Dr. Galloway arrived just as the urge to push wouldn't be denied. Cali held her breath as she propped herself to her elbows to bear down. The elderly doctor calmly examined Calista with a broad smile on his face.

"Well, I see the Mikos family is about to have its newest member join them. This little one is just about to make their appearance." He looked up at Andrea with a kind smile. "Are you ready to be a big sister, young lady?"

"Yes, sir." Her voice was surprisingly strong.

"Well, I think it's great you're here to greet your brother or sister. I'm sure you're going to be a big help to your mom and dad when the baby goes home, won't you?"

"Yes, sir. I already helped decorate the nursery."

Calista's heart pounded. The exchange temporarily distracted her from the all-consuming pain.

When Nick's phone dinged with a text from Katie's parents that they were there to pick up Andi, his eyes locked with Cali's. They silently communicated before she saw him respond back quickly. The decision was made—Andi was staying with them for the delivery.

Nick got up on the bed behind Cali, taking her in his arms, propping her body up, so she was supported as she pushed. He held her hands so she could squeeze when the pain got too intense. They gave Andi the job of wiping Cali's forehead with the cool compress between pushes. Nick's loving words whispered into her ear helped her stay calm when the pain threatened to overwhelm her.

"I love you so much, baby. You're doing so great. I'm so proud of you."

Fifteen long minutes later, Calista was exhausted and desperate for a rest that wasn't coming. The consuming pain never subsided, and she found herself begging.

"Please, Dr. Galloway. I give up. I need drugs. I can't do this anymore."

"I'm sorry, Cali, but it's way too late for an epidural. Your baby's head has crowned, and in just a few minutes, you're going to hold him or her in your arms. Let's give it a big push now."

Cali took strength from Nick and Andi holding her up, encouraging her with loving words, and she pushed until she was completely out of breath. Then it happened. She felt her baby slipping from her body as if a dam had broken. The intense pressure was gone, leaving a full-body ache that was forgotten as soon as the healthy baby's cry filled the room.

"It's a boy!" the doctor beamed as he announced. "Cali and Nick, you have a son. And you, young lady, have a brother."

There was a flurry of activity as the nurses rushed to take care of the newest addition to the Mikos family. Nick reached up to cut the umbilical cord, and within minutes, a baby swaddled in a baby-blue blanket was placed in Cali's waiting arms. She held him in one arm and put her arm around Nick who was moving in close with Andi for their first look at the baby.

Love flowed through Cali as she gazed down at the newborn in her arms. His shock of black hair contrasted with the splotchy pinkness of his skin. As his family looked down at him in awe, he opened his eyes and seemed to look directly into Cali's soul.

He was perfect.

"Welcome to our family, Alexander Nicholas," Nick's voice warbled with emotion. "We've been anxious to meet you."

As if he had understood his father's words, the baby looked at his sister and broke into a smile.

"Look Mommy! Alexander smiled at me!"

"I love you so much, Calista." Nick leaned into kiss Cali's forehead. "Thank you so much for bringing these two perfect babies into my life."

As she looked up at her family, Cali once again felt a peace she had only known for the last year. She looked lovingly into her husband's eyes as she answered.

"Don't thank me. Thank God. He's the only one who could have made this moment happen. We are truly blessed."

The End

THANK YOU FROM THE AUTHOR

I'd like to thank you for reading Blessed Betrayal. It would mean a great deal to me if you could leave a review or drop me a note to let me know what you thought of Nick and Cali's story. Feedback from my readers is how I continue to improve as an author. I'd love it if you'd check out one of my many other stories by visiting my Amazon page.

Never miss a release!
Sign up for my New Release Newsletter

Keep in touch here:
www.liviagrant.com
lb.grant@yahoo.com

EXCERPT FROM COMPLICATED LOVE

Emma's quiet "I'm sorry" was ridiculously inadequate for the hell she'd put the men through. As mad as he was at himself for letting things get so out of control, at that moment, all he could think about was her role in the day's shitshow.

Jaxson spun around so fast Emma flinched, burying her face against Chase's shoulder.

"You need to cool down," Chase cautioned, hugging their girl protectively.

"Whose side are you on? Ten minutes ago you were just as frantic as I was!"

"Since when do we take sides?" Chase snapped.

Fuck. He was right.

Jaxson ran his hand through his hair nervously. "That's not what I meant and you know it"

"The only thing I know is she's shaking like a leaf. We need to go in, sit down, and talk." Chase hugged Emma harder, speaking softly against her ear. "We were just worried, baby. Let's go snuggle and you can tell us what's going on."

When Emma didn't start moving towards the living

room, Chase bent down and scooped her into his arms. Jaxson watched as Emma wrapped her arms around his neck, burying her face against Chase's shoulder intimately, clearly feeling safe with the switch of their trio.

Watching his lovers comfort each other, for the first time in their almost three-year relationship a hint of jealousy threatened to poison Jaxson's already precarious thoughts. He pushed it down, knowing intellectually it was ridiculous, but recognizing it as just another sign of how out of whack things had gotten in their complicated relationship.

Still, as he followed behind them irrational anger bubbled through his veins, infecting him as surely as a virus. Months of crushing stress mingled with the day's events resulting in an almost out-of-body crescendo of emotion he had no idea how to contain â€" let alone shut down. A quiet voice in his head begged him to storm out and not come back until he was back in control, but the louder fury won the day.

"As much fun as it is to watch you two snuggling, we have a few more important things we need to be doing right now."

Neither Chase nor Emma answered him. Both staring at him with a healthy dose of fear in their eyes, making him feel like a line had been magically drawn between them. Him on one side, them together on the other.

He fucking hated it.

Fine. He was the Dom. It was his job to be the bad guy when the occasion called for it. "Emma, come here."

Her teary eyes widened. She glanced at Chase, deferring to him for advice. He hesitated, but finally nodded. "Go ahead, baby," he whispered as he helped her to her feet.

Emma approached him slowly, stopping just out of his reach. She was taking shallow breaths, unable to look at her Dom.

"Eyes," he ordered. It was an order he'd given her hundreds of times before in the throes of passion or in a D/s scene, yet today it felt different. It was different. Their unshakeable bond had a crack in it, and by God, he was going to figure out why and glue it back together.

Blurb:

Keeping two lovers in sync is hard enough. Three is incredibly complicated.

Jaxson, Chase, and Emma may have officially bit off more than they can chew. Already running two wildly successful clubs in Washington D.C., they decide to expand, opening Runway West and Black Light West in luxurious Beverly Hills, California. Â But there is no relaxing for the infamous threesome. With construction deadlines looming, staffing decisions to make, and multiple outsiders hitting on her men, Emma feels pressured into keeping a dangerous secret from them, breaking the number one rule of their unique relationship.

Can Jaxson, Chase, and Emma's complicated love survive all that life is throwing at them, or will the pull of outside influences cause it to fall apart forever?

Author's Note: Complicated Love takes place in the Black Light world and while the characters have appeared in previous books, it can be read as a standalone and complete story.

Pick up your copy here!

ABOUT THE AUTHOR

USA Today bestselling author Livia Grant lives in Chicago with her husband and furry rescue dog named Max. She is fortunate to have been able to travel extensively and as much as she loves to visit places around the globe, the Midwest and its changing seasons will always be home. Livia's readers appreciate her riveting stories filled with deep, character driven plots, often spiced with elements of BDSM

A Lovely Meal

Hero to Obey

Royally Mine

Just Breathe

www.ingramcontent.com/pod-product-compliance
Lightning Source LLC
Chambersburg PA
CBHW051945170626
46808CB00007B/2492